Manawl's Treasure

Manawl's Treasure

Liz Whittaker

Manawl's Treasure is the third book in
The Dreamstealers Trilogy

Book 1 The Fizzing Stone
Book 2 Shapeshifters at Cilgerran

Dedication:

To Joe Spiteri

First impression: 2005

Cover artwork: Jacob Whittaker
ISBN: 0 86243 785 7

Published with the support of the Welsh Books Council

y Lolfa

Printed and published in Wales
by Y Lolfa Cyf., Talybont, Ceredigion SY24 5AP
e-mail ylolfa@ylolfa.com
website www.ylolfa.com
tel. (01970) 832 304
fax 832 782

Preface

Two old tales were my inspiration for the Dreamstealers trilogy. The story in the Mabinogi of the Cauldron into which the bodies of dead soldiers were deposited to later emerge as Undead Warriors intent upon destruction was the first, and led me to create the monsters of the title. The second was the legend attached to the Gors Fawr stone circle in the Preseli Hills, where the Ancient Masters of Dyfed deposited all their spells in the hope that they would go to the 'Otherworld' and, in the process, lost them, and one of their number.

People have asked me whether either of the books: The Cauldron of the Undead, and Procton's Escalado, which appear in the trilogy, can be bought. They are, it must be said, a fictional device and exist nowhere outside the story; though you will find the story of the Cauldron at the end of this book.

Manawl, or Manawydan, (his full Welsh name) had a reputation as a great Wizard and Shapeshifter and has long been my greatest hero in Celtic Myth. He appears in the Mabinogi as a peace-loving, wise and magic figure; an unusual presence in stories of constant warfare.

The land of Annwn is Manawl's home. In myth, it is the land where the dead who have no reason to wish to be born again to this world, finally reside. It is, in other words, 'heaven' and the home of those who have 'graduated' from school-earth. For the purposes of the story, Dreamworld lies between this world and

Annwn and is a dimension so close to our own that it can be visited in sleep and in moments of psychic inspiration or perception.

I hope these details will enhance the reading pleasure for anyone who picks up this book and has not read the first two parts: The Fizzing Stone and Shapeshifters at Cilgerran

Liz Whittaker
Cardigan, August 2005

Chapter 1

The Final Task

It was cold and dark and Leo's feet were numb. He was fed up with waiting. He looked at his watch for the fifth time in less than the same number of minutes. There was no-one else at the bus stop and he was beginning to think he may have missed the bus back home to Narberth.

The trouble with choir practice for the inter-schools Christmas Carol Service was that, once a week, he was stuck here, on a deserted street in Haverfordwest, well after the time he should have been home and fed.

His stomach rumbled.

'I won't do it next year,' he mumbled to himself. 'My voice will have broken properly by then, anyway, and they won't be able to talk me into it.'

A sound behind him made him turn, and only just in time. He yelped in horror and made a sharp, instinctive leap aside, his bags scattering, as a baseball bat swung down past his ear, narrowly missing its target. His would-be attacker lost the bat and hurtled, sprawling, to the ground.

'What?' Leo gasped in disbelief as he realised who it was.

Bos Gribley, whom he had neither seen nor heard from for months, lay looking up at him, his face distorted with annoyance and hatred.

'I'll get you next time!' he shrieked, and, leaping to his feet, he lunged for the bat, which had rolled across the pavement.

Leo took a dive in the same direction and, grasping the bat before Bos reached it, he turned and waved it at him, with a threatening look.

'You could've killed me.' he cried. 'What d'you think you're doing?'

Bos didn't answer. He breathed heavily and glared at Leo, moving from one foot to the other as though about to launch another attack.

'You senseless idiot,' Leo continued, waving the bat to discourage Bos. 'You can't just go round whacking people over the head for nothing!'

Bos sprang at him even as Leo was speaking, forcing the bat from his hand and dragging him down onto the pavement. The bat spun away to where neither could reach it, and they tussled on the ground, trying to get the better of each other.

Despite Bos having taken him by surprise, Leo was bigger and stronger. After a brief struggle, he managed to overcome Bos and, holding him down, he pinned his arms firmly so that he couldn't move.

Leo was panting and sweating and genuinely scared, even though he was winning. He hated fighting. He never enjoyed it, like some boys did, and he was aware that Bos was serious, and really meant to harm him.

'What're you? Mad?' Leo shouted, and his voice was wild and angry.

Bos growled, pulled a disgusted face and, with a sudden effort, yanked his arm out from Leo's grip and clouted Leo a heavy blow behind his ear. Leo yelped as the sharp pain shot through his skull, and he couldn't stop himself swinging backwards and putting up his hands to his head.

This gave Bos the opportunity to scramble out and force Leo into lying on the pavement, where he could get on top of him.

'Right,' Bos hissed. 'Give it'ere. Now!'

'What are you talking about?' Leo grunted, writhing to free himself.

Bos was trying to go through Leo's pockets at the same time as holding him down, but it didn't work. Leo pushed him hard with his knees, sending Bos toppling sideways. Leo staggered to his feet and moved away warily, still facing Bos but standing well clear.

'What're you on about?' he repeated.

But he knew. He was only asking for confirmation. There was only one thing that Bos would want and, doubtless, he had been sent to get it by the same person who had wanted it the last time Leo had seen him.

It had been months ago, at the start of the summer holidays, when Leo and his step-sister Ginny had found themselves caught up in a race to find Manawl's brooch, a magical treasure left by the great shape-shifting wizard of ancient Welsh legend. The Dreamstealers, the ghastly freaks cooked up in the Cauldron of the Undead long ago, also wanted the brooch, to further their powers, and had enlisted the help of Bos Gribley.

They had very nearly carried the brooch away, with heaven knew what consequences, but by working with helpers from Dreamworld, who were known as the Dreamkeepers, Leo and Ginny had ended up winning possession of the precious object. Since then, Leo had seen nothing of Bos.

At the start of the September term, the headmaster had told the school that Bos's father had died and Bos had gone to live with his uncle. The impression given was that he had moved some great distance, a relief to everyone who knew him and to Leo in particular. But here he was, not that far away at all, alone with Leo, on a dark street in Haverfordwest.

He saw in Bos's eyes the same vacant look he'd recognised before, when Bos had been working with the Dreamstealer. He'd been robbed of his dreams. Now, no doubt the Stealer had sent Bos to retrieve the brooch, even if it meant injuring, or killing, Leo, in the process.

'Look at what you're doing!' Leo said, moving carefully towards the bat and watching Bos, who was now rising painfully from the pavement. 'Setting on people who've done you no harm, because somebody told you to do it.'

'You know what I want,' Bos said, but his voice was not confident.

He had fallen badly in the struggle and was rubbing his elbow; on his face was a look that suggested tears might follow. Bos's temperament was more suited to bullying than true fighting. He was a coward, as many bullies prove themselves to be when faced with genuine danger and discomfort.

'You mean what he wants.' Leo's voice was scornful. 'Don't think I don't know who you work for. Anyway, you don't seriously think I carry it about with me, do you?'

Bos looked confused. He had the vague air of someone who has forgotten what he is doing and finds himself in an unknown place.

'And why would you be helping him, anyway?' Leo continued,

remembering the threats the Stealer had made to Bos, when he failed to get the brooch for him on the previous occasion. 'He nearly killed you!'

Bos grimaced.

'He only pretended to do that,' he snarled. 'Anyway,'e just turned up again. And'e wants it. You know where it is. You gerr'it and give it us. If you don't...'

'What?' Leo asked, picking up the bat and swinging it gently. 'If I don't, what will you do? What did you think coming at me with a baseball bat would do? Did you seriously think it would be in my pocket, and you'd just grab it and walk away?'

He thrust a pointing finger at Bos, suddenly filled with anger and hatred.

'I'm telling you,' he breathed, 'if you come near me again, it'll be you that's sorry! Tell your Dreamstealer master that the first thing I did with it when I got home was put it into the dustbin. It's gone. It's been gone for months.'

Bos shrank. It was obvious that the thought of the Dreamstealer's anger at receiving such a message was a scary one.

''E won't like it.'

'I don't expect he will,' Leo said, 'but that's how it is.'

He wondered whether Bos believed the lie. Whether or not he did, it was the first thing that had come into his head and would have to do for the time being. He knew it was unlikely that the Dreamstealer would believe it, but maybe lying would give him a bit of time to think what to do next.

In the light of his previous experience of him, the prospect of any kind of encounter with the Dreamstealer was far more frightening than being attacked by Bos with a baseball bat. He felt a shiver of fear and an awareness of being alone, but he was determined not to show Bos what he was feeling. He continued to sound as casual as he could.

'It's not my problem,' he scoffed. 'I've got rid of the brooch. You can tell him I threw it away because I wanted to be left alone. It's logical, isn't it? Even you must be able to see that I got rid of it so he wouldn't come after me. No point. It's gone. Tell him.'

He shook the bat at Bos.

'And this,' he said, indicating the weapon. 'You're not safe to be left alone with something so dangerous. And I don't want it. So I might just take it to the police station.'

Bos jumped towards him, obviously intent on saving his bat, but Leo was quicker and, without a second thought, threw it over the fence that bordered the pavement, and into a small patch of derelict open ground behind it.

Bos growled.

'Go on,' Leo said. 'Get lost!'

Bos turned to walk away. He seemed to know his defeat was final.

'Tell him to leave me alone,' Leo shouted to Bos's back. 'And I've got friends, too. Remember them?'

Bos didn't turn, but Leo was sure he'd heard.

He hoped his words had reminded Bos of his one-time meeting with the Grolchen, one of the Dreamkeeper allies, who had broken through from Dreamworld the previous summer, to help Leo out of danger, when he and Bos had been trapped in the dungeon of Cilgerran Castle

The Grolchen, who had the appearance of a large cat with a human face and extensive bushy hair on his hind parts, had terrified Bos. But though he was a magical creature and definitely on Leo's side, he would not, Leo felt sure, have actually harmed Bos. But Bos didn't know that, and suddenly he seemed to change his mind about leaving and began to walk back towards Leo, smiling. He extended his hand as if offering to shake and be friends.

Leo was so stunned that he didn't respond.

'Listen,' Bos said, and his small mole-like eyes were like lasers aimed at Leo with a piercing beam. 'You could be rich.'E'll give you a fortune for it. Millions!'E don't care what'e pays for it. We could share it. Be wealfy. 'E'd have what'e wants. We'd'ave what we want.'

For a second, Leo wondered whether this was Bos at all, or whether it was indeed the Dreamstealer, whom he knew had the power to take someone's shape as well as their dreams. There was something hypnotic that rippled through him as he looked back into Bos's eyes. And, for a moment, he glimpsed how brilliant being a millionaire would be, and how good it would be not to have the Stealer on his back, and he thought, 'Why not just give it to him?'

But some part of him reared up, and he pulled his eyes from Bos's insistent gaze and looked down. The contents of his school bags, books and sports gear were strewn where they had landed when he had jumped to avoid Bos's attack. Now, they lay around him, littering the pavement. He began to pick them up and replace everything safely.

'But,' Bos continued, still staring at Leo. 'This is real money.'E wants it more than anythin'.'

'Are you all right?' asked Leo, keeping his eyes on his possessions and his bags and avoiding any contact with Bos's eyes.

'In the head, I mean? Or are you deaf? I threw it away! It was a dangerous thing. I haven't got it any more!'

Once his bags were secured, Leo slung one across his back and the other on his shoulder. He had just about had enough. If the bus wasn't going to come, there was no way he was going to stand arguing with Bos, or trying to avoid being hypnotised or beaten up. He began to walk, thinking to make his way to the next stop, to wait there, but, just in time, he turned and saw the bus coming round the corner. With a surge of relief, he waved to the driver, and, when the bus stopped, he jumped on board.

For a moment, he was gripped with the awful thought that Bos would follow, but he didn't. He just stood where he was, watching him, then, in a gesture which Leo couldn't understand, he raised his hand and, smiling like an idiot, waved Leo goodbye. Leo heaved a huge sigh as he took his seat. At least he had escaped Bos without harm, but knowing that the Stealer was on his trail and would not give up easily was a deeply uncomfortable thought.

He began to wonder why he shouldn't just surrender the brooch. What were his reasons for not handing it over? What did it matter, anyway, now there was only one Stealer left? What harm could one Stealer do, even if he did have hold of Manawl's brooch?

When there had been three, it was more difficult, of course, and the Dreamkeepers had a big job on their hands in keeping the balance so that good dreams didn't disappear into nightmares fed by the Stealers. It was fair enough to help them at the time. But now there was only one Stealer left, hanging around stealing dreams from innocent people, and there were still three Keepers.

Gido, the wise Welsh Professor, was their leader and it was he who detected the whereabouts of the wormholes through which the Keepers could travel from one dimension to another. Maria, the karate queen of his kitchen, was always alongside him, as was the Grolchen, whose music and listening skills were vital to their missions. In their first meeting with the two children, they had been trapped, prisoners themselves of the Stealers. Leo and Ginny had assisted them in escaping and, since then, they had helped the children against the Stealers' attempts to destroy their dreams and cause chaos and misery to their families and themselves.

Bos's attack made Leo aware that the remaining Stealer would never leave him alone as long as he had possession of the magic brooch. As the months had passed, he had hoped that the Stealer had given up and had lost interest. But, apparently not. It was time, he thought, for the Keepers to take care of matters. He would pass the brooch to Gido, when he could get hold of him, and if Gido would not take it, he would give it to the Stealer. He was fed up with being on the receiving end of all this trouble. It wasn't his problem and he wouldn't be pulled into it again.

The Keepers could either play their part, or Leo would simply hand over the brooch. The decision made him feel better. He couldn't understand at all why the Stealer wanted the brooch so badly, anyway. It seemed to have lost whatever powers it might have had last summer, and for months, resembling a small tin lid, it had remained in the bottom of a box of lead figures from Leo's Dungeons and Dragons game. He knew its real identity was a book of spells compiled by Manawl in ancient times. But, even in book form, it would only be useful if one understood how to use it, and Leo didn't think that the Stealer could possibly make it work.

He certainly didn't have any interest in making it work himself, though he had, at first, thought it would be quite exciting if it would do something. He'd tried the secret words Manawl had whispered to Ginny and himself, the words that were supposed to open the Defnydd Hud, the enormous book of spells locked within the brooch, woven into it by the master Magician in delicate threads of silver and gold. But, it had not transformed, or glowed, or felt warm in his hand, as it had in the summer. It continued to look like the lid from a tin of baby food; rough-edged, flimsy and with letters stamped into it. Leo had to admit it was a clever disguise and had even, from time to time, considered it might not be the brooch at all, but a genuine tin lid. Bos's visit had cancelled out that idea.

As the bus came to his stop and he was getting off, the driver spoke to him.

'That lad, the one you were with at the bus stop… friend of yours, is he?' he asked.

'No,' Leo said without hesitation. 'Why?'

'He's trouble,' said the driver shaking his head. 'Stay away from him would be my advice. Every driver on this route knows him. He bullies passengers and, whenever he can, he wheedles money out of the old dears. Makes'em feel sorry for him, and they end up giving him something, supposedly for food! He's a disgrace.'

He saw the look of disgust on Leo's face and nodded, continuing, 'Everyone knows his thieving ways. He'll get picked up by the police soon – mark my words. He's too stupid to realise that everyone's seen him nicking stuff off the backs of vans, in and out the shop back doors… you look like a decent lad. Don't go near him.'

'Thanks,' Leo said. 'I'll remember that.'

'He's bad news,' the driver said as he pulled away.

'Tell me something I don't know,' muttered Leo under his breath.

* * *

At home, the kitchen looked like a charity shop. Rhian, his mother, was working on the Christmas pantomime costumes for the local amateur dramatic society. Leo stepped warily through the heaps of fabric, hats and wigs, and grunted a greeting at his mother, who sat in the middle of a mound of taffeta, making Cinderella's ball gown.

She nodded towards the microwave oven.

'Sorry,' she said, through a mouthful of pins. 'Find something in the freezer. How did your rehearsal go?'

Leo had to throw off all thought of the Stealer and Bos's attempted attack and remember what he had actually been doing before it happened.

'It went okay,' he said. 'It's not really fair, making us do it after school, though. And why can't we practise at our school, instead of having to go to Haverfordwest? It's too late to do anything else by the time we get home.'

'Poor you. Never mind, it's the last one, and it'll be a real honour to sing at the Cathedral at St David's on Friday,' Rhian said. 'Ginny rang, by the way. She said someone you know has been in touch and asked if you would ring her when you came in.'

Leo sighed inwardly. He didn't need three guesses to tell him who Ginny was talking about. It must be the Stealer. Why else would Ginny ring him?

Ginny lived with her mother, Sara, in Cardigan. Her father, Carl, was now married to Leo's mother. Ginny and Leo went to different schools and had different friends but, together, they had shared the terrors of meeting the Dreamstealers and the Dreamkeepers, and Leo was sure that, after his meeting with Bos, Ginny would also have had some kind of visit. He selected an easy dinner, put it in the microwave, and rang her while he waited for it to heat up.

Ginny was breathless.

'I've had this really odd visit,' she said.

'Me too,' he said. 'Bos Gribley.'

'Oh, no!' Ginny paused as if taking in the information. Then, she said, 'Mine was Maria.'

'Really?' Leo was astonished. 'Maria?'

Into his mind's eye came the stout little figure with the wobbly bun and floral apron. Beaming with a constant genial smile, and with eyes like black-currants, no-one would take her for a Dreamkeeper. She cooked like a gastronomic queen and looked as innocent as a gentle granny, but she could aim a karate kick many men would envy.

'She came to me on the playing field at school,' Ginny continued. 'She wasn't fully here; you know what I mean, like she was made of water. She told me to watch out and not do anything silly.'

'I believe it,' Leo groaned. 'She's warning you that you know who's about again. Bos tried jumping me at the bus stop, with a baseball bat.'

She gasped.

'Are you all right?'

'Bit shaken,' Leo admitted. 'He came after the brooch. Said his friend would pay me millions.'

'What did you tell him?'

'I told him to get lost. I'd thrown it away.'

'Good,' she said. 'Yuk, that horrible boy! Just the thought of him turns my stomach. He smelled horrible and... well, anyway, I'm coming over on Saturday. For the panto, you know. We'll talk about it then.'

Leo did not have to be reminded of the date for the pantomime's opening night. It was etched in his brain as the day when the house would become home again, and not the favoured place for half the town to spend their social time. But today was only Wednesday, and Leo didn't want the threat of the Stealer hanging around him. He wondered seriously, for only a moment, whether he should do what he'd told Bos he had already done, and throw the brooch away.

He rejected the thought immediately. Although he wanted rid of it, he didn't want to be irresponsible about it. He must get Gido to tell him what to do with it. That was all there was to be done. Otherwise, he would insist that Gido take it. Then, the battle for it would be between the Keepers and the remaining Stealer. It had been lost for hundreds of years and, now it was found, he couldn't throw it away.

Gido had refused it, when it had been offered to him last summer, and Leo suspected he would do so again, but someone had to do something, or it would go on forever being a magnet for the Stealer. It occurred to him that it wouldn't be a bad idea to take a look at it. It was ages since he had done so, and it might possibly be showing signs of movement, since the Stealer was obviously about, and that is what had activated it on the previous occasion.

Something warm and tingly met his fingers, when he reached into the bottom of the box. Something was alive, reaching for his touch. It was the brooch and it was moving.

'Ye… s!' breathed Leo.

He withdrew it and gazed at it. The sight of it in motion filled him with the same amazement as the first time he had seen it happen. He felt a flutter of excitement. Something was going to happen. It always did, when the brooch began its extraordinary metamorphosis.

The way that it stopped feeling like a hard metal object and became fluid in his hand, the way that not only the texture but the temperature changed as it heated up, and then the glimmers and bright flashes that zigzagged like Morse code across its surface; all of this was warning that somewhere nearby was either a Stealer, or a Keeper, or some interesting magic happening.

'He will follow you,' said a familiar, quiet voice behind him.

In a way, though it made him jump, it was no surprise to hear the voice. If the Stealer was about, and Maria had already showed herself, then Gido, the Welsh Professor from the Keepers, would not be far away. Hearing the whisper from the shadows outside his bedroom window still sent a tingle up Leo's spine. He recognised the voice but could make out nothing visible.

'Watch him,' the voice continued. 'He has his spy out. But for now it is safe.'

Leo began to make out the figure of Gido, from the corner of his eye, as though reflected in the glass of the window.

'Outer circle,' murmured Leo.

'Quite right,' came the response. 'No point trying to come through properly – moon and planets in the wrong place entirely. You know, of course, that he is after you again.'

'Yes,' whispered Leo, holding the brooch and marvelling at the intricacy of the silver and gold wires snaking across its surface.

'You must carry it with you,' Gido said.

'No,' Leo said, and his voice shook. He didn't want to defy Gido, but neither did he want to be vulnerable to the Stealer's attentions. 'I'm going to put it somewhere for you to take it. We need to agree a spot.'

There was a moment of silence. Perhaps Gido was thinking of a place, or maybe he was just taken aback by Leo's suggestion, and didn't know what to say.

'No, no,' Gido said eventually. 'Please don't argue. Our line is weak - too little time. That is not the plan at all. Have no fear; your quest is almost complete.'

'So, what is the plan, then?' Leo asked.

The voice crackled and broke up, like a poor telephone line. Leo couldn't make out what Gido was saying, but he wanted Gido to be in no doubt about how he was feeling.

'All I care about is getting him off my back and off Ginny's back,' he said clearly and slowly. 'We can't use the brooch, anyway! I know you said you don't want it in Dreamworld, but we don't want it here either. We don't know what to do with it, and we can't just go on hiding and dodging him!'

'He can't hurt you!' Gido continued. The crackling had diminished and his voice had gathered strength. 'He can threaten, but why do you think he sent the boy to get it and didn't do the job himself? He can't attack you for the brooch. You must remember that from before. It is against the magic commandments within it. If he tried to rush at you for it, he would feel its force and be stopped. Your only threat is that boy.'

Leo felt himself getting annoyed. This was the same thing that had been said before, and seemed to suggest that he should be prepared to be under constant attack from Bos for ever more, and put up with it because in some way it was a privilege to look after Manawl's brooch. The brooch may well be a wonderful magical thing, but, despite the exciting feeling it gave him, he knew the constant risk was too high a price to pay for it.

'The Plan!' he almost shouted. 'You said there was a plan! I'm definitely not into Bos Gribley jumping me every time I look round, so tell me the plan!'

'Wait,' Gido said. 'And when the moment is right, READ. You know the source. The answer is there. As it always was. What was lost at Gors Fawr can be found in the Defnydd Hud. The final task is at hand.

There was a burst of loud static, and the window rattled as though a plane had whizzed by.

'You're talking in riddles again,' Leo said, and felt really angry with Gido. 'You're always doing it. Why won't you explain things properly? You want me and Ginny to live afraid all the time. Well, we won't. I'll chuck it away, if I can't find out what to do with it. So that's it.'

No answer. Leo moved his head, to try to catch sight of the figure beyond the darkness at the window, but it wasn't there. He wondered whether Gido had heard anything of what he had said, or whether, since he was travelling on the 'outer circle', the notoriously difficult way to transport between dimensions, he had simply been cut off before he'd heard Leo's ultimatum. Leo looked at the brooch again. It remained warm, but was completely still. Gido was gone.

Leo was about to replace the brooch in the box, moving the lead figures aside, when it twitched one more time. He stared at it and suddenly felt guilty. Gido must have felt it important to travel on the outer circle to communicate with him, and even if Leo didn't care for the instruction to carry the brooch at all times, perhaps there was good reason for it.

He changed his mind and closed the box. Carefully, he placed the brooch in the inside pocket of his fleece, where all he could feel was its warmth.

Chapter 2

Ginny's Visitors

Though Ginny had told Leo about Maria's unexpected visit, she had not told him what was happening when Maria had arrived.

In fact, until Leo told her the Stealer was about again, she had thought Maria had come to tell her off for being argumentative and risking her place on the athletics team. Why she should have imagined that Maria would go to the trouble of coming through from her own dimension to speak to her about something so relatively unimportant didn't occur to her. It just seemed that she arrived at a moment when Ginny was making a fool of herself, and Ginny thought she was trying to stop her from making it worse.

It was at the end of the weekly athletics training session, and the team captain, Gwen, disgusted at the generally miserable performance on the field, had turned on Ginny, whose new hairstyle, which flopped over her eyes, had proved a bit of a handicap. Gwen's criticism had been short and sharp, and that would have been the end of it if Ginny had been able to accept the blame. But Ginny liked her new hairstyle and was sensitive about her performance, which, if the truth were told, she knew hadn't been up to her usual high standard. So, in a moment of annoyance with herself and with Gwen, she turned on the Captain.

'It wasn't my fault,' she shouted. 'It was the mud!

As soon as she had yelled the words she knew she had done the wrong thing. Everyone stared at her. Nobody ever shouted at the captain. Gwen was well-liked and respected, and Ginny was being babyish and showing she couldn't take criticism. She wanted the ground to open up and swallow her.

Gwen walked off and left her to think about it, saying as she went that Ginny would lose her place on the team if she didn't buck up her ideas. At that moment, Maria's watery figure seemed to spin itself out of the air, and land lightly in front of Ginny.

Of the three Dreamkeepers, Maria was Ginny's personal favourite. Ginny knew that Leo admired Gido the most, and both she and Leo loved the Grolchen, but for her, from the moment she had seen the little housekeeper throw up her skirts and aim karate kicks at the Dreamstealer, Maria had been her heroine.

The sight of her now, appearing before her in the misty afternoon drizzle of the school playing field, was a shock, and she wasn't sure at first whether anyone else could see her. But since they showed no sign, not so much as a raised eyebrow, she gathered that they probably couldn't.

Most of the team were making their way across the field towards the school building, but Ginny stood, amazed and absorbed with the detail of Maria, real but unreal, who existed in another dimension, so familiar and so unknown, standing in front of her on the damp, windswept playing field, her wonky little bun bobbing up and down as she leaned towards her with a secret message.

Dusk was falling, and Ginny wondered for a moment if the small body was an illusion. It was drizzling and the floodlighting around the field was flickering as it prepared to come on. Maybe the weird light was making her invent the almost transparent figure. But then, Maria's words had tumbled through and Ginny was left in no doubt.

'Don' you go jumpin' into trouble, goin' beyond your ablin'. You watch out, my maid.' Maria said, and began to fade away and dissolve, even before her words had finished.

'What?' Ginny cried. But it was too late.

Maria had vanished and Gwen had gone, along with the rest of the athletes, across the field towards the school building. Ginny knew she had left it too late to apologise, and suddenly realised, thanks to Maria's warning, that if she lost her place on the team she might never get on it again. Her spirits sank. If she followed the others, as she should, back into school, she knew that Gwen could already have told Miss Davies, the Games teacher, about what had happened and, no doubt, if she had, Miss Davies would be waiting to give her a good talking to.

The thought of everyone listening in to Gwen blaming Ginny and her new hairstyle for the team's pathetic performance on the field was too much. Ginny squirmed. While she was still angry, she might argue, or, worse, burst into tears, and make herself look stupid again in front of them all. She stood on the darkening field alone, the drizzle creeping into her clothes as she agonised over what to do. There was no way could she make herself go indoors.

No, it would be much better to go straight home. It was, after all, the end of the afternoon and home-time, anyway. The problem of getting her bag and coat could be overcome by sneaking into the cloakroom through the rear door, which was usually open after practice. Then, she would just take off without a word.

Her friend, Jules, with whom she usually walked home, might

wonder where she'd got to, but she would go round to her house later in the evening and explain to her. She drifted back across the field towards the school building, melting into the shadows, and sidling along the wall to the rear cloakroom door. As she'd hoped, it was open, and furtively, like a thief, she crept in, grabbed her things and was gone before a soul knew she had been anywhere near. Once she was well out of the school gates and on her way home, she thought about how she would deal with it the next day. When she wasn't so upset and embarrassed, she'd go and apologise to Gwen, and try harder next time.

Athletics was her big thing. Next to dance, it was her favourite activity, and she knew she was the best by far in her year and one of the best on the team. She felt tearful and angry, all at the same time, at the thought that she might lose her place on the team.

She rang Leo as soon as she got home and, by the time he rang her back, she had calmed down and did not want to tell the whole circumstances in which Maria had appeared. She wanted him to know that she had been visited by the little Keeper. That seemed important somehow, but she didn't want Leo to know she had argued and made herself look stupid in front of the team, and that Maria had come to tell her off about it. But, of course, she hadn't come for that at all. Maria had actually come to warn her that the Dreamstealer was back on her trail, which only added to Ginny's feelings of gloom. On top of the prospect of being thrown off the team, it made her feel that life was being unfair.

A flood of memories swamped her, memories she would rather not have, of the times when she and Leo had struggled to keep away from the Stealer's power, to retain their dreams, and to survive the tricks he employed to try to turn them into Undead, like him. And now, he was back, and would be hanging around, lurking scarily, waiting for either of them to put a foot wrong.

It was all about that brooch, she thought miserably. She remembered how she had found it at Cilgerran Castle and not known what it was, but been sure it was something special. She wished now that she had thrown it away, but she couldn't because Gido had said it was important to find it and keep it.

It confused Ginny that nobody seemed to have any clear idea what they were supposed to do with it. She knew that it was magical and she had seen it change, but even though she knew that Manawl had given them words to enable them to use it, he hadn't told them what to use it for. And now, that horrible creature was back, looking for it, they were in danger, there was no-one to help them, and Manawl should have taken his stupid brooch with him when he went to Annwn!

All these thoughts ran through her mind and made her feel miserable and moody and in no frame of mind to write Christmas cards with her mum, which was the planned activity for the evening. When she came back from the phone after speaking to Leo, Sara, her mother, was sorting out cards and envelopes and lists on the big dining table.

The ritual of writing the cards always felt as if it brought Christmas suddenly to life, and every year they enjoyed doing it together. Ginny knew her mum would be disappointed if she said she didn't want to join in, so she flopped down on a chair and leafed half-heartedly through the cards.

'So, what did Leo say?' her mother asked, seeing the expression on Ginny's face, which was far from happy.

'Nothing,' Ginny said.

'Oh, nothing, was it?' her mother queried. 'Of course! People are always ringing up to say nothing, aren't they? Don't be a silly fibber. What did he ring for?'

'He was just asking whether I'm going with the school to St David's for the Christmas service on Friday.' Ginny said, grasping at the first thing that came into her head.

She could see that there was no way she could sit with her mum and go through the Christmas cards if there was going to be a quizzing of her mood. Her mother was very kind but Ginny felt she was being picked on.

'I've got a headache and I think I'll just have an early night,' she said, and though in a way it was an excuse, it was also true. She felt quite peculiar and shaky, and her head really was aching.

'He knew that already, didn't he?' her mother questioned, ignoring her and not giving up. 'He's in the choir. He told you he's in the choir and you told him your school were in the congregation, didn't you?'

Ginny didn't answer. She got up from the table, went over to the sofa and picked up the television paper. Her stomach had sunk in a peculiar way at the thought of the Stealer. Somewhere, very recently, in a dream, she had seen him, from behind and from a distance, but still that dark shape had been instantly recognisable. She reflected on it now, trying to remember the rest of the dream.

Was it a premonition? Should she have taken more notice of it? Maybe it was a warning that he was somewhere near, because, until then, he hadn't entered her head at all since the events in the summer. A fleeting image came back to her of that final day, when the river had swelled to claim the Stealer who lay, broken and unconscious, in the hands of Gido; and the other one, the remaining one, had stood shaking his fists and screeching at them. It stirred such a mixture of feelings in her that she couldn't concentrate on her mother, or Christmas cards, or even the athletics team.

'Did you have an argument?'

Ginny's head jerked up.

'Who?' she asked.

'You and Leo,' her mother replied.

'No,' Ginny answered.

Her mother eyed her with disbelief.

'Something's wrong,' she said. 'I know something's wrong. Come on. You can tell me, can't you?'

Ginny got up from where she was sitting.

'I'm fine, mum. I'm going upstairs to do my homework.'

'What?'

Her mother looked hurt and perplexed.

'You just said you had a headache! Anyway, you don't have any homework. You told me yesterday that they weren't giving you any homework so near the end of term because of all the other activities. Come to think of it, why were you home so early? I thought it was athletics today.'

'It was.'

'But you're always late after athletics – you are still in the team, aren't you?'

'We just finished a bit early,' Ginny said, and suddenly feeling the prick of tears behind her eyes, she made for the door and escaped.

'Ginny!' her mother called after her. 'Come back and talk to me...'

But Ginny ignored her and ran upstairs to her room. She closed the door and sank on to her bed, lost in a confusion of thoughts that would not go away. She waited a few minutes, in case her mother followed. Maybe, she should explain about Gwen threatening to throw her off the team. Her mother would be sympathetic if she didn't go into too much detail.

But no, even that was out of the question. Her mother would go on and on until she got the whole truth, and Ginny would get a lecture about being cheeky, and her mother would go on about her hairstyle, which she didn't like anyway.

But it seemed that her mother had decided not to follow. So, after a short while, Ginny got up and went to the window, to close the curtains.

The dark, wet evening was doing nothing to raise her spirits, and, outside, the rain had thickened from a drizzle into a downpour that rattled on the window. She glanced at the street lamp, which shone down on the puddled pavement, and, with a shock, she registered the shape of a man standing beneath it, looking towards the town. He wore a long, dark coat and a hat which, as Ginny watched, he pulled down over his eyes, but not before she recognised him. She had seen him, just exactly like this, in a dream recently.

She knew who he was, even though his back was turned and she couldn't see his eyes. How she knew it was him she had no idea, but there was not one scrap of doubt in her mind. And she was glad he was turned away from her. Once, two years ago, when she had first met him, she had almost yielded to his eyes. The thought of being caught in their gaze and turned into an undead zombie like him scared her stiff.

The Dreamstealer had found his way to her again, just as he had last summer. Maria's visit and Leo's call had given Ginny warning, and, thanks to them, the shock was not as great as it would have been if Ginny had been unprepared. Even so, it was alarming and frightening to realise that he was near, and that he evidently had some intention to get close to her.

She peeped through the curtain and saw that he was beginning to move off. He was heading down towards the town centre. Ginny wondered where he was going. Was he looking for someone? Planning some harm to someone else? Or was it for her alone that he had come? Her mouth had gone dry with anxiety, and her heart was thudding at the thought of him being right outside her door. Was he going to walk around town all night and wait for her to come out in the morning? Surely not; he must go somewhere, but where?

Maria had told her to be careful, and she would be. But the possibility of him hanging about, watching her, somehow changed her mood from feeling sorry for herself to feeling angry.

The anger crept through her and filled her till she simmered with outrage. How dare he come and frighten her? She would fight the feeling of being a victim. She wasn't going to lie awake all night, terrified of him, wondering whether he would be waiting for her in the morning.

With a sudden spurt of rage and a flash of determined energy, she turned from where she had been standing by the window and, before she could think about it, she ran from her room, slamming the door behind her. Snatching her coat from the banister post, where it had been thrown after school, she pulled it on as she took the stairs two at a time and flew out of the house, shouting to her mother as she ran.

'Five minutes, mum – just going over to Jules's!'

Then she was out on the front step, banging the door shut behind her.

She knew her mother would not think it unusual if she went round to her friend's house. Jules only lived round the corner and they often went to each other's homes in the evenings, to swap books and disks and share gossip.

For a moment, as she stood on the doorstep, a small inner voice invited her to go to Jules's instead. It would be easier and pleasanter than what she had in mind, and the Stealer, after all, had disappeared and was nowhere to be seen. But she silenced the small voice and took a deep breath.

She had spent too long being afraid, cowering from the horrible creatures. What was it Leo had said at the stones, when they had caught the first Dreamstealer?

'In films, they don't let the baddie chase them, they chase after him instead.'

That's what she would do. She would follow him and find out where he was going. If she headed in the direction she had seen him going, she thought she could catch up and stay just far enough behind to see where he went. Less than a minute had passed since she had seen him from her window, and she knew her way well enough into the town centre to keep in the shadows and out of the light from the street-lamps.

She set off, walking steadily in the direction she had seen him go. The rain was easing but there was a sharp wind and it was cold. She pulled her beany hat down over her ears, to keep out the sharp wind, and hunched lower into her coat. The main street ahead of her was well-lit and there were a few people about. She still couldn't see him, but he'd had a head start. She hoped he hadn't headed off down one of the small side streets. They weren't as well-lit and they were a maze she didn't want to get into.

'I'll just see where he goes, if I can,' she breathed to herself. 'Then, I'll report back to Leo.'

And it was at that moment that she saw him.

He was standing still, looking at the sky, his mouth wide open. He seemed to be drinking the rain. Ginny moved into the shadow of a shop doorway and watched. The man set off again after a few moments, and she slid after him, always keeping a good distance between him and herself, and staying, as far as she could, in the shadows. It confused her that he was headed towards the river.

The Teifi would surely terrify him. Neptune, Lord of the Sea, could easily capture him there. Perhaps he didn't know the town well. It would save them a lot of trouble if he did walk right to the river and get carried out to sea. But she knew he was too cunning to get caught like that. He'd been around for thousands of years. There was no way he would accidentally end up in the Teifi.

He was in Cardigan because he thought she might have the brooch. It was as simple as that. He wanted the brooch and he thought Ginny might have it, so he was hiding out here and would at some point appear before her and attempt to take control of her mind.

She swallowed a moment of panic. The desire to turn back suddenly gripped her but she mastered it. She put her hand into her pocket, where she had a small torch; she fingered it, reassuring herself that, though he was now moving downhill and away from the lighted shops and cafes into gloomier, shadowy areas, she could follow.

At the bottom of the hill, just before the chip shop, he turned and glanced back uphill. He paused, scanning the street. Ginny held her breath. Surely, he couldn't have seen her. Not clearly. Not well enough to identify her, even if he had caught sight of a movement. She was too far away and, in the moment he had turned, she had slipped behind one of the huge pillars outside the old courthouse book-shop. He set off again, and the relief Ginny felt made her realise how tense she was.

It crossed her mind that perhaps she should go home, but she was too intent and curious. What carried her along was the thought of how fantastic it would be to tell Leo where he was hiding, where his den was. Then, they'd get the Keepers to help, and they'd go there, find him, and Leo would use the brooch...

That was as far as her imagination took her. The shadowy figure did not turn again, and his slow stroll was replaced with quicker and quicker steps. But suddenly, he disappeared.

Ginny hesitated. She stood stock still for a moment, wondering what had happened. There was nowhere that wasn't within her view. Beyond the slope of dark roadway, the river, turbulent and foaming after weeks of rain, rolled away to the sea, and the glistening expanse of tarmac between was quite empty.

On the opposite side of the road were the ruins of Cardigan Castle, at the top of a high embankment. Massive, bright yellow, metal supports, which for years had stopped it dropping into the Teifi, leaned out across the pavement, and it was as Ginny's eyes roved upwards, taking in their size, that she suddenly saw the Stealer, outlined briefly against the sky.

He was climbing, balancing his way up the huge metal structure, and could only be making his way into the castle. At the top, she caught another brief sight of him as he leapt over the wall and, in one swift movement, he was gone.

She stood for a few moments wondering what to do next. The castle ruins were known to be structurally so unsound as to be hazardous, and were not open to the public because of their disrepair. Work was in progress to re-open them, but, for the time being, anyone in there was technically breaking the law.

She wondered whether she should go to the Police Station. It would be great to get them to go in and arrest him. But she knew from past experience that he may not be there in that form for very long. As soon as the moon's phase changed, or he chose to use his magic to become something or someone else, all would be lost. She would look totally stupid and the police would think she had made it all up.

A scuffle and muted bark made her look down. Beside her was her dog, Basil, a small, grey, silky creature with short legs and a long nose, who had obviously taken it upon himself to follow her. He was looking up at her hopefully.

'Basil! What are you doing here?' she scolded. 'Go back home!'

She waved a pointing finger back up the hill, but Basil, who was a well-trained animal and normally did as he was told first time, simply looked as though he hadn't heard a word she said.

'I could have found his den!' she moaned. 'If you hadn't turned up I could have got in there and watched to see where he's hiding!'

Basil continued to look at her as though she was out of her mind, a look he often cast her way when she refused to take him for a walk.

'Okay, okay, you're right,' she said. 'It would've been stupid. Better to wait for Leo, I suppose.'

So, with shrug of acceptance, she turned and began the walk home, feeling excited about what she would be able to tell Leo and what would happen when they managed to locate the Stealer.

But, if they found him, what would they do? They could hardly explain him to the police as a Dreamstealer. Even if he was breaking the law by living in the castle, they would only tell him off and send him on his way. And then he would be out free, and even madder with Leo and Ginny than he already was. Her mind seemed to be playing tricks on her, going round and round in circles, and her headache and the shivery feeling she'd had before had returned.

'I just need to go to bed,' she said to Basil. 'I've caught a cold or something.'

She would ring Leo, tell him what she had seen and ask him what to do next; that was the only sensible way to handle it. It felt good to know that she had something positive to tell him, though how they would use the information she wasn't sure.

She slipped indoors, with Basil behind her. Her mother looked up as they came in.

'I wondered where he'd got to,' she said. 'Then, I realised he'd probably followed you round to Jules's. I was going to ring to tell you to watch out for him, but, I thought, he knows his way back and he'll be all right without me fussing.'

Ginny breathed a sigh of relief. If her mother had rung Jules and found she wasn't there it would have meant explaining something she couldn't.

'Feeling better?' her mother asked.

'Not bad,' Ginny said.

'You don't look too good,' her mother said, putting a hand on her forehead. 'I think you've caught a chill. You feel like you might have a temperature. I suppose you were out on the field this afternoon, doing your running in the rain, weren't you?'

'Yes,' Ginny agreed. She didn't add, 'And I've just been standing outside in the freezing cold rain, watching a Dreamstealer,' but she thought it.

'Come on,' her mother said. 'I'll make you a cup of hot chocolate and you can get into bed as soon as you like. Have a good night's sleep. That'll do you the world of good. You don't want to have to take the day off tomorrow! You've got your Christmas quiz, haven't you?'

'I'll be all right in the morning,' Ginny said, with an enormous yawn. 'I just want to ring Leo...'

'Leave it for now,' her mother said. 'Get into your pyjamas and settle down. I did some cards but I wasn't really in the mood myself. So, maybe you can do your own when you want to, and I'll do mine while you're at school tomorrow.'

She pottered off to the kitchen to make the drink, while Ginny went to her room and put on her cosy pyjamas, soon warming up as she snuggled under her duvet.

Her mother was only minutes behind her, with a steaming mug and a couple of biscuits.

The comfort of the bed, the bliss of the hot drink, the relief of being warm and safe, all contributed to Ginny soon falling asleep, well before she intended, without ringing Leo to tell him of her discovery.

Chapter 3

Bad Act Bos

There were certain things that Leo knew he could never find out by himself. He remembered that once, right at the start of the mysterious happenings at Gors Fawr stone circle, he had found in the school library a book called The Cauldron of the Undead, which had helped him to understand who the Dream-stealers were.

Mr Evans, his class teacher at the time, had told him about it and, when Leo had discovered it in the library he had been fascinated by it. Mr Evans had said it was a rare book, no longer in print, and had seemed to be surprised that Leo had managed to get hold of a copy. It was only later that Leo found out the book belonged to Gido, who had 'lent' it for him to find and had later taken it back.

He wondered now whether Gido's almost shouted instruction to 'read!' meant that he had once again deposited the book for him in the school library. It was the only book that Leo could think of, aside from the Defnydd Hud itself.

He knew he couldn't read the Defnydd Hud. It only became a readable book in Dreamworld, so no-one could read it in the real world, where it existed as the brooch. Besides, he didn't think Gido was talking about the Defnydd Hud. He didn't know why he thought that, but he decided to use his intuition to follow Gido's riddle and see where it led him. At lunchtime on the day after Gido's visit, it led him to the school library, to seek the Cauldron of the Undead.

⋆ ⋆ ⋆

Mr Evans was in the library, and appeared to be cataloguing a new batch of books, which were heaped on a table beside where he sat at a computer, keying into a database. He was no longer Leo's class teacher but still taught him English, and Leo knew him as a good, interested teacher, who seemed genuinely to enjoy his job and like his pupils.

He smiled in a friendly way when he saw Leo come into the library.

'I hope you haven't come looking for The Cauldron of the Undead, Leo. We still don't have it!' he said.

It was meant as a joke, but it was such a shock to Leo that, for a moment, he stood with his mouth open. It was, after all, nearly two years since they had talked about the book, and it was as though Mr Evans had read his mind. It confused him, and feeling slightly flustered, he found himself answering, 'I thought you might have it in by now…' He tried to make it sound as though he, too, was joking, but something in the way Mr Evans looked at him made him wonder whether he had been convincing.

Mr Evans got up from where he was sitting and, beckoning Leo to follow, he took him to the shelves that held books on local history and mythology.

'What we do have, and I think you will enjoy,' he said, 'is this wonderful new series on Celtic mythology.'

He lifted one of the brand new, glossy titles out and flicked through it for Leo's benefit. Pictures of bronze helmets, golden torques, decorated pottery and arcane ritual items flashed across the pages. It was beautiful, but Leo knew it was not what he was looking for. Though he realised Mr Evans was trying to be helpful, Leo wished he would go back to his computer and leave him alone. If Gido had lent his book again, the last thing Leo wanted was for Mr Evans to find it before he did.

While they stood looking at the brand new book and Mr Evans enthused over the colour plates and the wealth of information contained in it, something kept catching Leo's eye. Pictures of standing stones and stone circles flew past with the turn of the pages, triggering an unexpected memory. When the class trip had visited Gors Fawr, he had been surprised to find that Mr Evans had known the legend of the stones, a tale that said that this was the place where the spells of the ancient Druid Masters had been buried.

Gido's words, 'What was lost at Gors Fawr,' came back to him, and in a moment of sure insight, Leo knew that what he really needed to read about was Gors Fawr, not the story of the Dreamstealers.

'You remember when we went to Gors Fawr stone circle?' he asked Mr Evans now. 'Is there a book with the story you told us in it? I remember reading it in a magazine, but it was only a bit, not a lot of background or anything.'

'I'm pleased you're still interested,' Mr Evans said, and he looked thoughtful for a moment. 'I think it was you who suggested that we go to the stone circle, wasn't it?'

'Yes,' Leo said. 'And it was a really good day out.'

'So it was,' Mr Evans agreed. 'Have you been again since then, at all?'

Leo shook his head.

'Nor me,' Mr Evans said. 'Perhaps in the Spring, I might…'

He was running his finger along the row of books and he withdrew a slim blue volume.

'Here we are,' he said. 'This is a collection of local stories and legends, and some of them are just as interesting as that one, but I'm afraid you won't find Gors Fawr in there. To my knowledge, it isn't in any book at all.'

'So, how did you know about it?' Leo asked.

Mr Evans pondered.

'Someone told it to me,' he said. 'I think it was someone who lived near the stones. I liked the story so much that I remembered it.'

'So did I,' Leo said, but he was disappointed. 'I rather thought that there might be more details, things I had missed. If someone told it to you, they must have read it somewhere.'

'Not necessarily,' Mr Evans said. 'It may well have been one of those local legends; what the historians call 'oral tradition' – never written down, just passed on by story-tellers. Why are you so interested? Are you thinking of using it for creative writing? I seem to recall you wrote something very good about it before; a sort of fantasy tale, wasn't it?'

Leo nodded.

'I'm thinking of turning it into a play,' he said with a flash of untruth that seemed to come to him out of nowhere.

Mr Evans laughed as he turned to go.

'Best of luck! Could be difficult,' he chuckled, 'getting sixteen standing stones on the stage!'

He went back to his work, leaving Leo to browse the shelves. He flicked through the book Mr Evans had given him, but it was all about ghost stories and tales from a hundred or so years ago; nothing in it of the kind he wanted. He replaced it on the shelf and ran his eye over the entire length of the shelf again. There was nothing that jumped out, that looked as if it might mention Gors Fawr, so he checked carefully, just in case the Cauldron of the Undead had magically appeared, but it hadn't. He turned away, deflated, and was about to leave, thinking he had probably got Gido's clue wrong, when Mr Evans returned.

'This might help,' he said, holding out a somewhat tattered old book. 'It's Procton's Escalado, the only book that lays claim to knowledge of the worlds between worlds. Old Procton was thought to be a madman when he wrote it, but so many of his prophecies and his wisdoms have been proved right that people are revising their ideas of him. I'd forgotten, but I have a feeling he mentions the stones, though I don't think he tells the legend in full.'

Leo recognised the name of the book as one of those that Mr Evans had talked about at the same time as he had recommended The Cauldron of the Undead. He held out a hand to take it from him.

'This is my own copy,' Mr Evans said, as he passed it to Leo, 'and so, I'm afraid I can't let you take it away. It is old, valuable, and, indeed, more than valuable to me. In fact, I would go so far as to say it is precious with a capital P. So, you may use it now, here, if you wish, and if there is anything useful in it you will just have to copy it out.'

'Thank you, sir!' Leo said, filled with a rush of gratitude and the sudden certainty that exactly what he needed to know was in this very particular book.

'I happen to have it here with me because I have been doing some research myself,' Mr Evans said, as he sat back down to his work.

Leo took the book and sat down at one of the tables between the rows of shelves. He opened it at the back, and looked through the index, running his forefinger down the lists, seeking any reference to Stone circles, or Gors Fawr, sure he would find something, but there was nothing.

His elation evaporated, and he was about to close the book and return it to Mr Evans, when he thought of looking up Druid, for which there was a string of page references and, just below, following it in the index, was Dyfed Masters. The very sight of the words made the hairs on his neck rise, and he knew he had found what he was looking for.

It was a bite-size piece of about twenty lines, and Leo copied it down as quickly as he could. It took him longer than he expected. It was strange, old fashioned spelling, and he didn't understand anything of what it said. He felt a small thrill when he saw Manawl's name in the paragraph. This looked promising if difficult. He knew he would need to read it closely later, but, for now, he wanted to get back to his classmates.

There was so much to talk about, with Christmas less than a fortnight away. His best friends, Greg and Loll, would be wondering what he was doing. They might even start thinking he'd become a swot, spending all his lunch hour in the library. He had intended to come into the library, make a quick search for the

Cauldron book and leave, not spend ages copying ancient words from a barely decipherable passage in a book that looked hundreds of years old.

'Did you find anything?' Mr Evans asked, when Leo finally returned the book.

'Sort of,' Leo said. 'Not the legend, but something.'

He didn't want to say he didn't understand it, in case Mr Evans decided to start on a long explanation.

'Interesting that I should have it with me,' Mr Evans observed, 'since I have never brought it into school before. I can only think you were meant to find that piece of information today, Leo.'

Leo paused. A part of him wanted to leave, but his curiosity wouldn't let him go without asking a question.

'Do you believe in things like that?' he asked.

'Like what?' enquired Mr Evans. 'Synchronicity? Destiny at our elbow? Forces that serve us but are beyond our understanding? Of course. I have seen so many of such moments in my life, I would be an idiot to try to deny them.'

'You mean coincidences?' Leo asked.

Mr Evans nodded thoughtfully.

'Yes,' he said, 'with an edge of something special!'

'What are you researching?' Leo blurted out the question despite himself.

'It would be difficult to explain,' Mr Evans began, and Leo wished he hadn't asked.

But the teacher seemed to sense Leo's eagerness to depart and, instead of launching into a long explanation, he shook his head.

'Some time, when we have more time, I will tell you about my research,' he said. 'But for now, perhaps you should make the most of what is left of your lunch hour, before it disappears.'

Leo grinned, murmured his thanks and left.

He caught up with Greg and Loll as they lingered at one of the school's outside doors, watching the weather and commenting on the unlikely prospect that snow might come along and put paid to the afternoon's lessons. They agreed that there was definitely the feel of snow in the air. This led to a discussion of what they would do if it snowed in the holidays.

Leo found himself longing to take out the piece of paper and read it. He realised that, until he had read it properly and understood what it meant, he would be restless and uncertain, and he might as well have stayed in the library and reread it and, maybe, asked Mr Evans what it meant.

Later, after a long day at school and a final rehearsal for the concert the following day, he arrived home. The words on the paper were still uppermost in his mind. It seemed as if the more he thought of the encounter with Mr Evans and his book, and the teacher's assertion that he must be 'meant' to find it, the greater its importance seemed.

But first, he was starving. The kitchen was once more in chaos and the freezer yielded the same boring selection as the day before. He began to feel disgruntled and, in an act of rebellion after his makeshift evening meal, he took a tub of toffee-crunch ice-cream, which he knew should serve at least two people, and managed to make his way through it. Whilst he polished off the giant portion, he was thinking.

A number of thoughts preoccupied him. Mr Evans and the Escalado; the curious passage about the Masters; Bos's attack of the night before; Gido's message; Maria's visit to Ginny; and, finally, he wondered whether the brooch, which was currently still in his pocket, would ever find its rightful home if it wasn't wanted by anyone at all. It had been twitching on and off since lunch time, and he was looking forward to getting it out in the privacy of his room, to see if it was changing.

It had occurred to him that his idea of forcing Gido to take the brooch by threatening to give it to the Stealer, was stupid. Giving the brooch to the Stealer would simply remove any security that he and Ginny had, and the Stealer could hardly be relied upon to show gratitude.

The doorbell rang, loud and persistent, breaking his train of thought. He shook his head at the thoughtlessness of the person on the doorstep. It was, no doubt, an anxious member of the pantomime cast his mother was expecting, arriving to pick up a finished costume for the dress rehearsal the following evening. He ignored the rude, insistent chime. He was planning to stay well out of the way of any visitors, and disappear upstairs to his own room, where he could consider his problems in peace.

He really wished he could talk properly to Gido, but, failing that, he was going to have to try to find out more about Gors Fawr, and see what Gido had been getting at. If there really was a plan, it was hopeless to expect to be able to carry it through with Gido fading in and out on the outer circle. Getting in touch with him properly was the only answer and, if the words from the Escalado offered some clues as to what to do next, so much the better.

After a final, regretful lick of his spoon, he made his way through the hall as the doorbell rang again. Leo took no notice of it and began to climb the stairs. Rhian bustled out of the sitting room into the hallway.

'You might have answered it,' she said to Leo, a little crossly, on her way to the door. 'As if I haven't got enough to do!'

But Leo was taking the stairs two at a time and didn't answer.

It was with a shock of disbelief that he heard the voice at the door, a voice he recognised, that stopped him in his tracks.

'I'm sorry,' came Bos's whining tones. 'I've fallen an''urt myself and lost me bus fare'ome. I'm a friend of Leo's'

Leo stood transfixed and appalled, as he heard his mother invite Bos in, clucking round him with all the anxiety of a mother hen.

'Come in, come in, you poor boy. Oh, dear, look at your eye...'

She ushered him into the hallway and looked up the stairs, to where Leo stood staring.

'Your friend,' Rhian beckoned him. 'He's hurt! He needs to borrow some bus fare to get home. Hang on, I'll get my purse.'

'No, no, I don't want no money for fare. It was the last bus,' whined Bos. 'I can't gerr'ome now. I live in'Averfordwest, see... the last bus's gone.'

'Oh, dear!' Rhian said. 'Shall I ring your parents and get them to come and pick you up?'

'Me uncle,' he replied. 'I live wiv me uncle. Me mam an' dad are dead, an', no, me uncle don't drive, so'e can't pick me up.'

He said it with all the tragedy he could summon, and Rhian's face showed that she was filled with sympathy, but was concerned to know what to do next.

'Oh, you poor boy,' she said.

Leo felt cold. What was Bos up to? He certainly had a huge,

shining, blue-black bruise around his eye, and he looked dishevelled and upset.

Rhian looked from one to the other. She saw Leo's distaste. She also saw what an awful boy this 'friend' looked – rough, cold, hard-edged somehow, in spite of the pitiful whine in his voice.

'What's your friend's name,' she asked Leo.

'Bos,' Leo answered, and even to himself it sounded more like a croak than a voice.

To Rhian, the name meant nothing but it told her that Leo knew him, so, presumably, they were friends and, maybe, the boy was telling the truth.

'I'll see if Carl might give you a lift. I'm afraid I can't – I've too much to do,' she said, turning to go.

'If I could ring me uncle an' just let'im know where I am,' Bos said, 'it would save'im the trouble. I could stay the night'ere and get the bus first fing in the mornin'.'

Rhian looked at Leo, unsure what to say.

'No way,' said Leo, but it came out so quietly that Rhian thought he hadn't spoken and was simply standing staring at Bos as though he couldn't believe his eyes.

Confused and not sure what to do next Rhian made a decision to go for assistance.

'I'd better go and find Carl, see if he can help,' she said and disappeared.

When she'd gone, Leo came down the stairs and scowled at Bos.

'Yesterday, you tried to smash my head in, and suddenly, I'm the only place you can stay,' he hissed. 'Get lost.'

Bos frowned and pointed to his eye.

'This is what'e did. Cos of you,' he said. 'An' I get another an' another till you give me that… that… medal thing. I'm bruised all over, so I'm not scared to fight you for it, or you can just'and it over and'e won't touch me again.'

'You'd lose if we had a fight,' put in Leo quickly. 'You know you would. Just get lost. Run away from him. He can't control you. Get away from him and leave me alone.'

'I can't,' Bos said. 'I can't.'

He looked at his feet as though he might suddenly burst into tears.

'Look,' Leo said. 'Why don't you just get a lift with Carl and go home to your uncle's and…'

'You did this,' Bos said, pointing to the eye.

Leo was finding it hard not to be sympathetic, and he resented it. Bos's eye looked painful and all because Leo wouldn't give him the brooch. It made him feel guilty and angry all at the same time.

'No! I didn't,' he said. 'He did it!'

Rhian returned with Carl just as Bos waved a threatening hand at Leo, shouting, 'It's all your fault!'

'What is?' Carl asked, in his usual calm way.

''e nicked me torch,' Bos said, turning to answer Carl, the lie dropping so smoothly from his lips that it left Leo gaping.

'I was just sayin,' continued Bos. 'that if'e'adn't nicked me torch, I wouldn't'ave fallen, but…'

Carl may have been listening to what Bos was saying, but Leo could also see that he was weighing Bos up, looking at him in a curiously interested way. He went close up to him and, whilst nodding as though he was taking in everything Bos was saying, he walked round him and then stared into his face. Leo almost giggled. It went through his head that it looked as though Carl was auditioning Bos for a part in the pantomime, his eyes searching every bit of him.

Maybe he was trying to make Bos feel uncomfortable for some reason. If that was his intention, it seemed to be working. Bos was shifting from one foot to the other, his eyes flicking from side to side, as though he was wondering what was going on.

Carl put out his hand and very gently lifted Bos's chin, so that he could get a look at his bruised face from a different angle under the hall light.

'Fallen, you say?' he said. 'Oh, dear, you must have come quite a cropper.'

'Yes,' Bos continued, but Leo could see that Carl's scrutiny was beginning to make him feel nervous.

He shuffled a bit to move away. Carl let him.

'I slipped and fell down and my'ead'it this bollard thingy,' Bos said. 'It, like,'it me in the eye with a thwack.'

'Did it?' asked Carl. 'And that's when you lost your money?'

'Yeh, I'ad it in my'and an' I dropped it. It rolled away an' it was dark an'...'

'So, it's bus fare you're after?'

Bos looked as though he was tired of repeating himself, but he started again.

'I don't want no bus fare. I need a bed for the night.'

'Because you fell?' Carl was close up again, examining the bruised face.

Bos nodded.

'No. Try again,' Carl said, and he looked up and winked at Leo.

Leo was startled. What on earth did Carl mean by winking, when it was obvious that Bos's face had suffered some awful damage? Had Carl somehow worked out that Bos had been thumped and hadn't fallen at all?

Carl continued staring at Bos.

'So, why are you really here?' he asked quietly.

'What?' Bos thrust out his chest. 'You sayin' I'm a liar?'

'Yes, I am, as a matter of fact,' Carl said.

Bos wrung his hands, and the whining tone returned to his voice.

'I thought you'ad nice parents,' he said to Leo. 'I thought they'd'elp me.'

'I think someone hit him,' Leo said to Carl, feeling he should speed things up. 'He didn't actually fall.'

'No. He didn't fall, you're right. But he wasn't thumped either. Were you?' said Carl, and his voice had taken on a sterner tone. 'Maybe we can help if you tell us the truth, but the fact is, you're lying at the moment, and I can't help wondering what this little performance is all about.'

'Why would I lie?' Bos cried. 'Look at me!'

'I am looking at you,' Carl said. 'That's how I know you're lying.'

Leo looked again at Bos's face, and wondered what Carl was seeing that he hadn't seen himself.

Carl started to chuckle, shaking his head. Bos's silence was embarrassing. He reddened under their collective stare.

'I do the make-up for our drama company,' Carl said eventually, folding his arms and smiling at Bos, as though inviting him to come clean. 'I even went on a course to find out how to make realistic bruises and injuries. Yours isn't even very well done. What did you do it with?'

He came in closer and squinted at Bos's face.

'No, don't tell me, let me guess. Oil, pastels? Or, maybe, boot polish and lipstick. So what's it all about?'

There was a moment of shocked silence.

Then, to Leo's horror, Bos flung out his big booted foot and gave Carl a sharp kick in the shin. Carl let out a howl of agony and clutched his leg as he toppled. Rhian shrieked and ran protectively towards him. Leo jumped at Bos and tried to grab him.

It all happened so unexpectedly and took them so much by surprise that Bos was too quick for them, and, elbowing Leo out of the way, he was out of the door and running away before anyone could stop him.

Leo was furious. He couldn't remember ever having been so angry with anyone. Bos had succeeded in tricking him, had led him into feeling sympathy and guilt with a bit of make-up! How stupid could he have been, to fall for that?

He wanted to run out after Bos and drag him back, to apologise to Carl for hurting him, and to himself and Rhian for deceiving them. But Carl saw him heading towards the front door and shook his head.

'Let him go,' he said, rubbing his shin. 'He's trouble. Is he really a friend of yours?'

'No,' Leo said fiercely, for the second time in two days. 'He's definitely no friend of mine.'

And at that moment, in through the open front door came the first two of the pantomime players, beaming cheerfully and looking hopefully for their costumes. Rhian welcomed them and directed them to the sitting room, then instructed Carl to go to the kitchen and put a bag of frozen peas on the bruise.

'You'll have a lump the size of an ostrich egg,' she said. 'Leo will get the bag out of the freezer for you.'

Carl hobbled away to the kitchen, where he sat rubbing his shin whilst Leo got the bag of peas out. When Carl rolled up his trouser leg, it was evident that what Rhian had said was true. There was a nasty bruise swelling up, and Leo felt a terrible sense of responsibility for Carl having been hurt.

Carl looked at him as though he was expecting Leo to tell him what was going on, but Leo couldn't think how to explain Bos's visit, and he could feel the brooch twitching under his fleece, which made him want to get to his room to see what was happening to it.

'Nothing to add?' Carl asked. 'I mean, it isn't every night that a nutter with a painted face turns up, asking for somewhere to sleep.'

He chuckled and waited. Then, as the frozen pack touched the bruise, he winced.

'You don't have to tell me, of course,' he continued. 'But I have a feeling there's bad business between you.'

'He's an idiot,' Leo said, turning to go. 'I hate him and I don't know why he came here, or why he did that. I just wish he hadn't. I'm really sorry…'

'Not your fault,' Carl said. 'You know what I thought?'

He pointed to the side of his head and, twirling his finger in a funny gesture, he said, 'Struck me as a bit twp,'

Leo managed a grin. 'Twp' was the local Welsh word for short on brains and barmy, and was the perfect description of Bos. If

Carl thought Bos was twp, he wasn't blaming Leo for the incident, which was a relief.

'He is definitely twp,' Leo said. 'The trouble is, he's a bully as well as an idiot.'

Carl was quick to size up the possible problem.

'Is he bullying you?' he asked.

'No!' Leo answered, but he was conscious of blushing as the baseball bat incident came back to him, 'but he is a pain.'

'Any problems, just ask,' Carl said. 'I mean it. Okay?'

'Thanks,' Leo said.

'No problem,' Carl said. 'Now, you go and get on with what you were doing. I'm fine.'

Leo left him and retreated back up the stairs to his room. He could feel the brooch moving like a live thing in his pocket, and he was dying to see what was happening to it. He sat on his bed, held it in his palm and watched it, mesmerised. Where there had been the dull grey of a tin lid, now the surface ran with what looked like molten silver and gold. Beneath the surface, yet quite visible, were flashes of colour, streaks of light, like the veins of a mineral hidden far down inside a stone, throwing up an occasional bright spark of orange, blue, purple or white.

'It's like electricity and it's definitely doing something,' Leo muttered to himself, 'and I'm sure it means I should do something, but I don't know what.'

He thought back to when he and Ginny had used it before. She had seen words in the brooch, and when she spoke them, Manawl had appeared, a ghost from Annwn. Perhaps, he pondered, Ginny having called up a ghost should have terrified them, but it didn't. He remembered it now as an astonishing and magical happening, like catching sight of an angel. He lay back on his bed, holding the brooch above him, looking up at it with the overhead light behind it, to see if he could make out any words.

Nothing.

Maybe, he needed Ginny to interpret it. The thought came into his head and stuck there, and he could tell that it wasn't his own thought, but had somehow come from holding the brooch. So, the brooch needed the two of them to activate it properly!

He continued to watch its activity, and thought about contacting Ginny. There would be no point in doing it on a school night, when they couldn't get together till the week-end. She had said she was coming over on Saturday, so he would see her then, but to find a way of getting together before then was impossible.

He knew she would be at St David's the following day, for the Carol Service, but he wouldn't be anywhere near her school contingent. He would be up in the choir stalls and she would be somewhere miles away, at the back of the cathedral, amongst hundreds of other Cardigan pupils. He replaced the brooch in his pocket, then, he changed his mind and put it under his pillow. Maybe it was safest for now to keep it as close to him as possible, even when he was sleeping.

Chapter 4

Weird Happenings

If Thursday had been a frustrating day for Leo, it was a day of disasters for Ginny. She woke with a throbbing head and a runny nose. Her mother seemed uncertain whether she was well enough for school and, Ginny, glad of the chance not to have to face Gwen and Miss Davies, and the added possibility of running into the Stealer outside the door, claimed to be feeling worse than she truly was.

A day under the duvet was preferable to being told that she had been thrown off the athletics team, or questioned about why she had left without reporting back into school at the end of the session. It was certainly better than bumping into a zombie with burning eyes turned on her.

'You'll miss the Christmas quiz, won't you?' Sara asked. 'I think it's only a cold. You might feel better if you get up, and you were looking forward to today, weren't you?'

'No,' moaned Ginny. 'I feel awful.'

So, though her mother eyed her suspiciously, she tucked her in and brought her some breakfast in bed and, after eating it, Ginny went gratefully back to sleep. She had not slept well the night before. The Stealer's presence had filled her dreams, and variously, throughout the night, she had run from him, faced him, and even taken a gun to find him. There was more, which she could not remember.

But now, with daylight coming in through the half-drawn curtains and her mother downstairs, humming as she busied herself, she felt safe and she slept soundly and dreamlessly. When she woke, it was mid-day. Her mother took her temperature, declared it normal and suggested that she get up and have some soup. Ginny then spent the afternoon writing her Christmas cards and, at around five o'clock, Basil started fussing for his daily walk.

'I'd better take him now,' Sara said. 'It's a nuisance because I wanted to get on with the plant bowls I'm doing for Izzy and Bella for Christmas, but he won't rest if he doesn't have his walk.'

'I feel quite a bit better,' Ginny said, perking up. 'Let me take him for you.'

'Not when you've been in bed half the day!' her mother said. 'D'you want to catch another cold right away?'

'No, honestly, mum,' Ginny said. 'I do feel much better and you said my temperature was normal. I could take him with me to post my cards and then go round to call on Jules and find out how the quiz went. That'll be a long enough walk for him.'

Sara dithered. The kitchen sink and worktops overflowed with plants she had nurtured from seeds, now in various states of flowering and foliage. She would love to continue and see her task finished by this evening. Each antique pot, carefully chosen from boot markets in the summer, would hold a profusion of growth produced from Sara's green fingers for her two sisters.

'Okay,' she said, giving way to her enthusiasm to see the gifts completed. 'But don't go further than that, and wrap up well. It's freezing out. And you must go back to school tomorrow. It's the last day of term and you're going to the Cathedral. Promise me. If you're well enough to go out, you're well enough to go to school.'

'Promise,' Ginny said, and she meant it. She had no intention of missing the trip to St David's, and if she had to find out she was off the team, it would be better to know before she broke up, rather than spoiling the holidays, worrying whether or not she'd been dropped.

She pulled on her warm sweatshirt and favourite fleece, her hat and gloves, then clipped on Basil's lead.

'See you in a bit,' she said to her mother, suddenly giving her a hug for being so kind.

She meant what she had said. She really did intend to go to Jules's straight from the Post Office. She was anxious to find out whether any mention had been made of the events of the previous day, and she was looking forward to a gossip with her friend, to put more scary thoughts from her mind.

But something happened as she stepped out into the dark street. Just as she had closed the gate to the little front garden, she turned and caught sight of the Dreamstealer, under the street lamp, only yards from where she stood. As he had on the previous evening, he stood as though waiting for someone. Then, he set off down towards the town centre, as before, at a steady, though in no way hurried, pace.

A mixture of terror, anger and tiredness swept through her. It was almost tempting to turn back, to run from the sight and kid herself she hadn't seen him. But she couldn't. She hovered for a fraction of a minute. Then, looking down at Basil, she tugged his lead and began to follow. Basil planted his feet firmly on the ground, and stood determined and defiant.

Ginny stooped and hissed into his ear.

'Are you coming or not!'

Basil tugged the opposite way. Ginny took the loop of his lead and tied it to the gate.

'Right,' she said in her sternest voice. 'Stay there, then. I won't be long. I've got to see where he goes. If he goes to the castle again I'll know for sure he's got a den in there, and I can tell Leo.'

She turned and walked away, trying to keep sight of the disappearing figure. Basil let out a bark of dismay as she left him.

★ ★ ★

Bos's attack, and his ridiculous charade with the make-up trick, played like a record through Leo's mind again and again. If things were going to go on like this, with something happening every day, he wanted to get rid of the brooch as quickly as possible. The trouble was that, when he saw it doing its amazing starlight effects, he didn't want to part with it – ever, even if he never found out what to do with it.

He knew that until he made an effort to find out what Gido wanted him to do, Bos may well keep turning up. The thought reminded him of the piece of paper and its mysterious contents, which he had copied from the book. He opened it and scrutinised it, taking it line by line, trying to overlook the weird spelling and just looking for the sense it made.

'Where lieth the tear in the veil?' he read. 'The Maesters of Dyfed, Cantref of Magic and Illyusion were counted those few who sought destinate to the Eternal Quest and did travail to persue the teaching of the Great Manawydan, the only humane bethought to have it discovered. Mistaken in both persuasion and numeral calculation their act of Hystoric follye did cause them suffer their life's final end and millenia of Devine teachings and alchimical texcts were swept from man's reache to the ocean's depthe. Suche can be saide the rewarde of pitting man's feebel ends against the Guardians of the Many Kingdoms who, in their mercy, do seal the doors of our petty livyngs against the knowing lest we fall to madness and psychic disorder. For who can looke beyond the boundarys of nature's own aurder without the highest of wisdome and of motive? Theirs was an act borne out of feayr and hatred. Did ever either of these most despycable and weak of human failinges bring any illyumination to celybrate into the world of matter and elevate man's journie to those undiscovered horyzons which do lye beyond our own?'

Leo read and re-read it. He wished he had taken the time at least to glance at what had gone before and after it. Whether that would have made it easier to understand he wasn't sure, but this seemed so bleak and condemning, and it left him feeling more confused than ever.

The mention of Manawydan, the old name for Manawl, the original designer and creator of the brooch, suggested that the great wizard of ancient times had, at some time, had knowledge of how to access another world. The Masters had misunderstood, and had died, and caused serious loss to the world.

Gido's message ran through his head again. Up until he read the piece, he had considered the action of Gido and his friends at Gors Fawr to have been an act of generosity to the world. When Mr Evans had told them the story at the standing stones, he had made it sound as though it was a wonderful act of heroism.

The Masters had thought that they were sending their magic and wisdom to another dimension, so that it would not become corrupted, and because they believed it to be dangerous in the wrong hands. Now, he was seeing it from a different viewpoint, because he was sure this was what it was talking about.

Procton, the writer of the book, obviously thought they were wrong in what they did and that their motives were anything but good. Leo wondered how this new piece of odd information fitted with what Gido had been getting at with his talk of a plan. Surely, Gido had been suggesting that Manawl's brooch could retrieve what the Masters had lost…

But how?

At some point in his thinking, when he seemed to be going round in circles, he looked at his watch and registered that it was getting late, and he should start thinking about bed. He knew that the following day at the Cathedral would be a long one, and that he needed to be in good voice. He heard the telephone ring downstairs, then the murmur of Rhian's voice answering it. There was a sudden babble of shrieks and raised voices, both Carl's and Rhian's.

After a few moments, Rhian's voice called him. 'Leo! Come down.'

Pretty sure it was Bos on the phone, making another rubbish attempt to get to him, Leo got up slowly. He didn't want to speak to Bos again. He had definitely had enough of him for a long time.

'What? What is it?' he called.

'Now!' shrieked his mother. 'Get down here. Ginny's gone missing!'

Leo leapt from his room in alarm. His legs shook beneath him as he ran downstairs.

Rhian was in a state of panic, though she tried to appear calm.

'Ginny's mum, Sara – she's on the phone,' she said. 'Ginny's disappeared. She went to see a friend earlier and never got there. Sara thinks you might have said something to her last night...'

Racing through Leo's head went all the possible things he could say to avoid mentioning what he knew. It was the work of the Stealer, or Bos, he was sure.

'They've been looking for her for the past three hours,' Carl said, looking worried. 'I'm going over to Cardigan now. Sara wants a word...'

He thrust the phone into Leo's hand and dashed off to find his coat and get ready to leave.

'Hello,' Leo said into the phone.

'Leo. Tell me what happened when you rang last night,' came Sara's worried voice.

'Not a lot,' Leo swallowed. 'I rang to see if Ginny was coming here after the concert at St David's on Friday. It's the pantomime on Saturday, so I wondered if she was staying over.'

There was a silence.

Then Sara said, 'I'm very scared Leo. You must understand that. If there is anything you can tell me that might help... you didn't fall out did you?'

'No,' Leo protested. 'Not at all.'

'Her friend Jules,' Sarah's voice was shaky, 'says someone told her Ginny got into trouble at school for something yesterday, and walked out before home time. Then, this morning, she wasn't very well. She'd caught a chill so I kept her at home. I thought then it was a bit odd. She's not usually reluctant to go to school, and it was only a cold. Then, this afternoon, around tea-time, she felt better and I let her take Basil for a walk to the post and to her friend Jules's. I was really cross with her because she was out such a long time.'

She stopped to cough, but Leo could tell she was doing her best to hide the fact that she was trying not to cry, and he felt terrible for her.

'So I went to the front door,' she started again a moment later, 'just to take a look if she was about, and there was Basil, barking himself hoarse, tied to the gate. I hadn't heard him because I was in the back of the house. So, I rang Jules's home and she hadn't even been there.'

'Is there anywhere else you can think of that she might have gone?' Leo asked.

'No, nowhere,' Sara said. 'And what makes it worse is, it turns out that she didn't go there last night either, when she said she did. So, where did she go? She's never done such a thing before, gone off and told me a lie about where she was going. And she was so moody after the phone call with you. You would tell me if there was anything, wouldn't you? Did she tell you what happened at school?'

'No,' said Leo hastily and truthfully. 'She never mentioned anything to me.'

'She wouldn't run away. Would she?' continued Sara fretfully. 'I asked her what the problem was. I knew there was something worrying her last night, but she wouldn't talk to me. Did she sound all right to you on the phone?'

'She sounded okay,' he said warily. 'A bit flat, maybe. Didn't Jules have any idea what she was in trouble for?'

'No. She hasn't seen her. I did ask her why she was home early, because after athletics she's always late! She seemed quiet when she came in, but I just thought she wasn't very well, and she didn't really clam up on me until after the call with you. Are you sure you didn't say anything to upset her?'

Guilt and anxiety ran through Leo. Of course he'd said something to upset her. He'd told her the Stealer was back. But that wouldn't make her run away, not Ginny. And that was yesterday.

'No, no,' he said. 'Could she have gone to a different friend's house? I mean, maybe she said Jules, but meant someone else...'

'There's no-one else who lives just round here,' Sarah said. 'Jules is her only real friend and, anyway, that was hours ago. I can't understand where she could be, and why did she leave Basil tied up outside? That's what concerns me most. He would look after her, you see – I'm sure he would. Oh, I'm so worried...'

Carl had reappeared, muffled against the weather.

He beckoned for the phone and Leo passed it to him.

'I'm on my way,' he said into it. 'Ring me on my mobile if she turns up, or ring Rhian. I'll be there within the hour.'

He replaced the phone with a thump and, giving Rhian a peck on the cheek and a farewell salute to Leo, grim-faced, he left the house.

Silence spread between them as it sunk in.

'Oh my God,' Rhian whispered. 'What's happened to her?'

'I don't know,' Leo said. 'But it might be nothing. It's only...' he looked at his watch, 'twenty to eleven. She might have met someone she knew, and just be hanging about in town. Maybe she didn't mean she was going to Jules's; p'raps she went to a different friend.'

But his voice sounded hollow, as though he didn't believe a word of what he was saying.

'Leo, she isn't going to be hanging about town, when she's been in bed with a cold all day, is she?'

His mother looked at him and sighed, pulling herself upright.

'I'm going to carry on with what I've got to do; sewing on sequins. You are going to put your stuff together for tomorrow, and then get off to bed, right.'

'But…' Leo was about to say he might be able to help, but then what could he do?

'I won't be able to sleep,' he said.

'I know, love,' his mum squeezed his shoulder. 'None of us will, till we find her.'

Leo trudged back upstairs. Somehow, he knew that Ginny's absence had something to do with the Stealer. He'd sent Bos to get the brooch, and he'd been unsuccessful, so why not move on to Ginny? Whatever the Stealer was up to, it was the brooch he wanted, not Ginny in particular. But perhaps he saw her as a means of getting to Leo. He wondered whether the Keepers knew what was going on. Did they know where Ginny was?

Before getting into bed, he slipped the brooch from under his pillow and held it fiercely in his hand, clutching it like a magic talisman. The brooch was slightly warm, twitching, as though poised ready for action.

'Please,' whispered Leo, staring out of his window at the dark, freezing cold night. 'Keep Ginny safe, wherever she is.'

★ ★ ★

Ginny dreamed of Gido.

He was telling her how difficult it was to reach her with the help she needed. His face and voice, familiar from their previous adventures, was somehow soothing as it reached her in the restless, uncomfortable half-sleep she was enduring. But his words were anything but comforting.

'If you had only listened to Maria...' Gido was saying. 'She did try to warn you...'

'I know, I know!' Ginny murmured.

'The scope of the task we face whenever we come to you is, by human standards, jaw-droppingly difficult,' Gido was saying. 'Moving between dimensions from dream-world into your dense material world, involves dangers which you cannot begin to imagine. Maria stretched herself to come to you. We could see he had you in his sights.'

'But I need help,' the dream Ginny said, 'not a lesson in how stupid I've been.' She felt herself near to tears.

'We're aware of this,' Gido said, 'but Maria suffered to come to you, and we can do very little more until the moon and Neptune dictate. The Stealer aims to capture the brooch, which must not happen!'

The dreaming Ginny wished he would say something helpful. Then she saw the Grolchen in her dream, and he was stamping his feet as though he, too, was impatient.

She became excited and pointed at him.

'Send the Grolchen! He got Leo out of the dungeon before, and he could get me out of here now.' Then she remembered and added, 'Except, I don't even know where I am.'

'Mic, Mic,' the Grolchen called, but Gido shook his head.

'He nearly lost his way last time he rode on the outer circle for Leo. Grolchen, being a creature of dream, risks the possibility that he might get caught inter-dimensions and dissolve, disintegrate…'

'Oh, shut up!' the dream Ginny shouted. 'Stop explaining hard things to me. I don't want to know!'

'I am not trying to make you feel worse than you must already be feeling,' the dream Gido said. 'But whatever happens, we must stop our enemy getting his hands on the brooch. His power would be increased. At the moment, he cannot take life, though he can pollute it. If it falls into his hands he could cause death and mayhem.'

Ginny began to cry in her sleep. It was too much to think about.

'I want to get out, just to get out. That's all.' she sobbed.

And the waking Ginny tugged at her bound hands, and the dream began to fade.

'We will do our best,' Gido was saying. 'emit htiw repmat ot yrt lliw ew…'And his voice disappeared.

Ginny heard his final words and, somehow, despite the fact they sounded like rubbish, her half-asleep brain understood that they were simply back to front. But how could Gido do what he promised? And suddenly her eyes were wide open, and she could see nothing but deep darkness. Her hands were tied together and her eyes were blindfolded. She yelled aloud, this time fully awake, conscious and afraid.

'Help!' she yelled. 'Help, someone come, please, help!'

No-one came. She wondered where she was, and, wherever it was, how she had fallen asleep.

She raised her bound hands to the blindfold and tugged at it. It would not move, but at least she could feel it was only made of fabric of some kind and not something she had dreaded. The thought brought her up short. What was it she dreaded? She knew that if she could remember it would tell her where she was. Her brain moved slowly, painfully, back to before the dreams and the uncomfortable sleep. She had left Basil tied to the gate and set off into town, following the Stealer, keeping out of sight but keeping him in view.

Exactly like the night before, she had watched him climb into the castle, and then she had turned to make her way home and... She struggled to think what came next. She was walking round the corner and something happened.

There had been a sound, the whirring of wings. Looking up, she had seen the bats emerging from within the castle walls, swirling outward in a stream of dark shapes, filling the evening sky with fluttering wings and the squeaking, rustling sound they made when they were setting out for the night. The sight had made her stop and stare. Against the night sky and with the backdrop of the Christmas lights along the river Teifi, it was like a magical synchronised dance, a procession of hundreds of small creatures in a gradually unwinding winged spiral, as they parted and went their separate ways. And for the first time, it occurred to her that, though the castle had been empty of humans for years, it had been the home to an enormous family of a very different kind.

She had laughed with pleasure and followed their flight with her eyes. And as she stood, head back, gazing, one of them, larger than the rest, had detached itself from the others and, turning in its flight, had flown straight at her. She saw, briefly, a pair of glowing eyes, out of place in that tiny bat face, and she had known who it was, and in that moment, she had tried to close her mouth, look down, and run.

But before she had chance to escape, it had landed like a clamping hand, covering her mouth so no sound could emerge. Then, reaching upwards with its wings like groping fingers, it had covered her eyes. She couldn't see, she couldn't breathe. She could hear the pounding in her chest and then she had fainted.

The memory, as it returned, made her head spin, but she gritted her teeth and made herself think further into what had happened next. She remembered nothing more but she didn't think she was still outside on the pavement. She could hear the wind but couldn't feel it, so she was definitely indoors somewhere. It wasn't warm, but it was sheltered. She was half-lying, half-sitting, propped against a wall, on what felt like a thin, hard mattress.

He must have brought her into his den, and she would still take a guess that it was somewhere inside the castle walls. Most probably, she was within the ruins of Castle Green House, which stood at its centre. The thought gave her little hope. Though she had a rough idea of the lay-out of the house, having visited it one open day, just before the council started work on the restoration of the castle grounds, she knew that no-one was working on it in the bad weather. There was no likelihood of anyone else being about.

She could find her way out if she could get the blindfold off, of that she was sure. She raised her hands, to try again, and as she tugged at the blindfold, she felt the binding on her wrists begin to slip.

She wondered what time it was, and then she heard movement, as though someone had joined her. Her instinct was to yell, to make herself heard, but, somehow, she knew that it was not the right thing to do, and so she bit her lip and stayed quiet.

'If you are awake, then be warned,' said a cold familiar voice. 'You are my guest, and if you insist on shrieking and shouting, I shall cover your mouth. If, however, you stay quiet, then, as soon as I have the brooch, you will be released.'

It was him. Ginny shivered but she continued to focus on her wrists, working them gently within their bindings, to free her hands.

'I know that you don't have the brooch,' the grating voice continued. 'If it was on your person I would have been unable to get close to you at all. And, remember, I was not following you. It was you who were following me. All I was planning to do was to reach out and see if, in passing, I might touch your person.'

Ginny knew this was a lie. He had led her deliberately, knowing she was following.

He continued to talk. 'That way, I would have known whether or not the brooch was with you. But, as it happens, this turn of events is fortunate for us both. The boy will know I am serious about claiming what is rightly mine, and you will have learned a valuable lesson in life. Can you guess what that might be?'

Ginny didn't answer.

It sounded as though he was on the far side of the room from Ginny, and the edge of spite and anger in his voice didn't encourage her to speak.

'The lesson would be to mind your own business,' he continued. 'Your inquisitive nature brought you here, and you have given me a bargaining tool I could not have hoped for!'

There was a noise somewhere else, somewhere outside but near, within the grounds. It sounded like people calling to one another, and it was obviously unexpected to the Stealer. He made an impatient 'tsk… tsk… ing' sound, and she heard him leave the room, presumably to investigate. Ginny strained to hear but the voices were no longer there. Maybe, whoever it was had been farther away than she thought.

She continued to work her hands and, as she moved and twisted them, she could feel herself growing freer. She stopped when she heard his steps returning.

'When someone comes for you, it will be because they have given me the brooch and I have told them where you are,' he said. 'And I will be far away.'

He waited. It seemed as though he was waiting for Ginny to speak, to protest, to answer back, but though she could think of many things she would have liked to say, they were all guaranteed to make him angrier than he was.

In her lap she felt a sudden release, as one hand, then the other, slipped out of their confinement. Her hands were quite free. She wondered for a panicky moment if he could see what she was doing, or whether it was too dark. But the Stealer was too busy talking and boasting to be watching her efforts closely.

'If I had the time, I would remove your blindfold and you would, despite your best efforts to resist, become my agent,' he crowed. 'But why would I waste my time on one such as you, who would fight me all the way, when the world is full of others, who will welcome me into their lives at a mere glance? Once, you were a dangerous enemy; now, you are simply a stupid child. The brooch will be mine and my power will be unmatchable anywhere. Should you then ever come near me again, you will feel a wrath you cannot imagine.'

Ginny could think of no response that would not endanger her further, and so she stayed silent.

'You think you have worked for good?' he went on. 'You think, by taking up with the Welsh Professor and his cronies and fighting me, you do good. You think you have done a good deed, ridding this world and Dreamworld of my brothers?'

He paused, but before Ginny could answer, the voice continued. 'Whatever you choose to believe, there is little difference between us,' he sneered. 'Keepers and Stealers we are called, but we are all trapped in the space between worlds. They pay for their own wrong-doings; we pay for the wrong-doings of others. Gido is clever, cleverer and more cunning than you can know, and, in the end, they are the same as me. They are using you, you and your young hero friend.'

Ginny made herself think of other things. She thought of Basil and her mother. She thought of Jules and her other school friends. And she told herself over and over that she didn't believe a word of what he said. She knew he was lying, and she didn't want to hear what he was saying.

'They, like us, are between life and death,' he continued. 'Stuck in Dreamworld, and you are their only means of redemption.'

Ginny's skin crawled as she suddenly became aware that his voice had drawn nearer and she could feel his breath on her.

'My only interest is in the brooch,' he said. 'Nothing more. And now I know you do not have it, I know who does.'

Then he saw her hands.

'What have you been doing?' he demanded, and lifted her untied hand.

She gulped.

Then she heard him laughing. He was laughing as though he couldn't stop.

'Foolish child,' he said, when his laughter had subsided. 'It will make little difference. There are superior bindings at my disposal, which is why you slept so long.'

He began chanting a string of words. It seemed as though he kept repeating the same thing over and over, until her brain couldn't bear the sound of it any longer, and such a longing for sleep came over her that she was unable to fight it. Her head lolled forward as she let herself go into nothingness.

* * *

Friday morning arrived, with Leo bleary-eyed. He had spent a less than easy night's sleep and was anything but eager to go to the Carol Service at St David's. He knew he couldn't miss it but it was the last thing he wanted to do. Imagine going to sing hymns and carols, when he felt so rotten about Ginny. It didn't even cheer him to think it was the last day of term. He just wished he could be out on the streets, searching for her, like Carl was doing.

As he came downstairs, the phone rang and he leapt for it at the same moment as Rhian jumped up from her breakfast and ran towards it, but he got there first.

It was Carl.

'They've found her, they've found her, and she's fine,' he said, and his voice sounded relieved and tearful all at the same time. 'Put Rhian on,' he said.

Leo passed the phone to Rhian, and hung about; knowing he might miss his bus but determined to wait and hear what had happened.

She turned when she had finished speaking, and spontaneously hugged him.

'Oh, Leo, thank God,' she kept saying, and he found himself hugging her back.

A huge lump of emotion was stuck in his throat, and as he pulled away and watched her weeping with relief, he realised how scared they had all been.

'She fell,' Rhian was saying. 'She fainted when a bat landed on her face. Can you believe that? It died on her face! It must have been flying when it was dying; but of all the places to do it! Can you imagine, poor girl, she must have passed out and been lying there all night.'

'What?' Leo asked, and his brain was working overtime, trying to figure out whether this could be something to do with either the Stealer or Bos, but not sure what the possible connection could be. 'Could you tell me slowly please?'

'That's all I know,' Rhian said, wiping her eyes and pulling herself together. 'God! Look at my mascara! What a wreck. Anyway, that's all I know. She was found lying in the undergrowth by the castle, with a dead bat on her face. They think she must have fainted when it hit her, and she was semi-conscious when they almost fell over her, so they took her straight to Cardigan Hospital, but she was fine when she came round fully. I can't believe it. It's just such a huge relief. I don't know what I thought, but I didn't think anything like that. I mean, who would think of that? A bat, for heaven's sake?'

'But what was she doing at the castle?' Leo asked. 'I thought she was supposed to be going to Jules's house?'

'She told Carl that she was walking down to look at the Christmas lights over the river, before she went to her friends house, and, suddenly, the bats came out of the castle and one of them just smacked her in the face. Then she must have passed out and lain there all night. She must have been in deep shock. I've never heard of anything like it. She's lucky not to have hypothermia, it was so cold last night. Poor kid, what kind of a weird accident is that?'

The word 'weird' was one of Ginny's favourites too, and Leo found himself thinking, whilst Rhian continued to ponder and prattle, that, in these particular circumstances, it was very descriptive and exactly right. It was certainly weird enough to tell Leo this was not something that had happened by accident, and, if he knew anything at all, that bat had been something to do with the Dreamstealer.

He wished he could go straight over to Cardigan and find out, talk to Ginny, and see if there was anything he could do, but he knew that he had to get to school and then to St David's. Suddenly, he knew he would sing his heart out in the Cathedral. The relief that filled him made it possible for him to do his best at anything today.

He reached the bus stop with seconds to spare. It was drizzling, a fine cold rain that felt as though it might turn to sleet. Despite the miserable weather, his school-friends were cheerful, full of talk about the forthcoming holiday. Leo was so relieved about Ginny being found, he launched immediately into telling them how she had gone missing the night before, and been found that morning.

His audience was stunned by the thought of the bat coming in to land and to actually die on someone's face. There was a good deal of swooping around and waving of arms and laughter to set fear to one side.

'But what did it feel like? Yuk!' someone said.

Leo found himself wishing he could ask Ginny that very question. He wished he didn't have to wait until the following day, when Ginny was coming over for the pantomime. The day stretched ahead, and he wondered how he would get through it all.

As it happened, he was so busy that the time flew by. The service was a great celebration of Christmas songs and music. The choir sang so well that the choirmaster was over the moon with pride and couldn't stop smiling. Their singing was followed by the enactment by children from a local primary school of the story of the birth of Jesus in the stable in Bethlehem, and Leo found himself genuinely happy to be there. When they bowed their heads to pray, he said a silent thank-you for Ginny's return. Someone was on their side, and he felt it right that, since he had asked for help, he should thank whoever was responsible.

The anticipation of Christmas approaching was in the air, and there were smiles and friendliness everywhere. The pupils in the congregation filed out happily at the end, and headed back to their buses, to return to their various schools. They chattered noisily as they went, feeling that school holidays were almost started. The choir remained behind to hand in the surplices they had worn for the occasion and to receive their special programmes, to remind them of the day.

Leo was almost the last to leave and, outside the doors, he breathed the December air with a shock. It had been cold when they had gone in, but it had now grown suddenly even colder. The rain had turned to sleet. Snow could be on the way.

He began to climb the wide stone steps towards the road, and turned to look back. The Cathedral and the ruined Bishop's Palace alongside stood below him. With the sleet coming down between him and the buildings, they appeared to float like a magnificent image from a fantastic film set.

Leo wondered how anyone had come up with the idea of building such a remarkable edifice in this remote setting, on the edge of land and sea

He was taken with the same awe that had filled him the first time he had seen it, when he was on an outing with his mother, and she had told him about the hundreds of people: builders, craftsmen, painters and monks, who, centuries before, would have been working on this monumental structure as a tribute to God. Its precision and beauty held him like a spell and he wondered, not for the first time, if one day he would be a historian.

It was a pleasant moment, shattered when he lowered his gaze to observe someone coming up the steps, following him.

'Cold, innit?' Bos leered, as he approached.

'What're you doing here?' Leo demanded.

'Waitin' fer you,' came the reply. 'Came in with the school kids.'

He jerked a thumb towards a group of pupils making their way up the stone steps towards the road. Leo had no idea what school they came from and thought Bos probably hadn't either, even if he had come on their bus. Before he had a chance to ask Bos which school he was going to, since he had left Leo's school, Bos had come alongside him and muttered into his ear, 'Just thought I'd pass on the message. I knew you'd be'ere. Give it me now and she goes free. That's what'e told me to say.'

Leo looked at him with a long appraising stare.

Bos was a wreck. His clothes were so grimy, they looked as though he buried them each night and dug them up in the morning. Or, maybe he just slept in them. He smelled of rank uncleanliness and of drink.

'You stink,' Leo said. 'And you've been drinking.'

'Little drinky in the pocket,' nodded Bos, as though he was proud of his stupidity. He reached into his pocket and held out a small hip-flask. 'Whisky,' he said, with a cocky smirk. 'Want some?'

'Don't be an idiot,' Leo said, and started to walk away.

Bos grabbed at his arm but Leo shook him off.

'Yer'll wish you never done that,' Bos grunted. 'I know where'e's got'er...'

Leo suddenly felt so angry with Bos, he could hardly think.

Bos had certainly had something to do with Ginny's so-called accident, but was obviously unaware that Ginny was now safe and well at home. But before he gave this information to Bos, Leo wanted to find out as much as possible of what had happened

'I don't know what you're talking about,' he said. 'Ginny's fine.'

Bos shook his head.

'If you fink you'll trick me into tellin' where she is, forget it. I in't tellin' you. No chance. But'e says'e'll let'er go when'e gets what'e wants. An' what'e wants is the brooch, as'e calls it.

It don't look like a brooch. Women wear brooches, don't they? That what you'ad looked like a medal. Anyways, whatever it is, that's what'e wants.'

'No idea what you're on about,' Leo said, and now that he was in control of his anger, he was beginning to enjoy taunting his enemy. 'Actually, I wasn't strictly accurate. Ginny isn't fine. She's got a bit of a cold, so she hasn't come today. She's at home with her mum.'

Bos looked at him with an expression that suggested he wasn't sure whether to take Leo seriously, or whether to simply explode with laughter and continue with his threats.

'All'e wants...' he started again.

Leo sighed and shook his head.

'So you keep saying,' he said. 'But to be honest, I'm not interested. Ginny is not in danger, and unless you count being jumped on by you from time to time, neither am I. I told you before, I don't have the brooch, anyway, but I think you might find that things have changed since you took your last instructions.'

In his pocket, the brooch twitched gently, reassuring him of its presence.

'What you on about?' demanded Bos. 'I seen'im yesterday an''e told me to watch you and'e'd watch'er, and'e went off to Cardigan.'E got'er.'E told me.'E got'er.'

'Sure,' said Leo, and seeing the pupils from his school heading towards the transport, he made to go to join them.

'Where you goin?' bellowed Bos angrily. 'Your sister's bin kidnapped and you don't care...'

'I wouldn't say it too loudly,' said Leo. 'I could easily call a policeman. Look.'

He pointed to the top of the road, where two uniformed policemen were standing talking, obviously attending to the unusual amount of traffic and bodies about.

'I'm sure they'd be pleased to know that you're part of a kidnap attempt. Oh, and that you're drinking under-age, and in the cathedral! You want to watch yourself.'

They stood facing each other aggressively across the steps, and Leo thought for a horrible moment that Bos was going to lunge at him and try again to snatch the brooch from him. But, at that moment, a man in the clerical robes of a priest drew parallel with Bos on his journey up the steps. He looked from one to the other and immediately sensed their mutual hatred.

'Trouble, boys?' he asked mildly. 'Not on a day like today, I hope. Today is a day for forgetting our differences and making friends. Come along now, whatever the problem, it can be solved by shaking hands in a spirit of forgiveness and Christmas.'

He looked Bos up and down in what could have been pity or shock, Leo couldn't tell. It was a difficult moment. There was no way that Leo wanted to shake hands with Bos but there was this nice man, who knew nothing of what went between them, and Leo wasn't sure what to do. He didn't want Bos anywhere near him, certainly not near enough to reach into his pocket and do something sneaky under the pretext of making friends.

The priest took Bos's arm in a movement of encouragement.

'One step is all it takes,' he said kindly.

Neither of the boys moved.

The priest sighed and let go of Bos, shook his head, and continued climbing.

Leo mumbled an apology to him as he passed him, then, turned to follow him.

He would feel better when he was back on the bus, with his school friends around him.

'Hope I don't see you around,' he said over his shoulder to Bos, leaving his enemy staring after him with an expression of deep puzzlement and frustration.

Chapter 5

Bos Tries Again

'What happened?' Leo's eager query came as he helped Ginny to carry her bags upstairs. It was Saturday afternoon, and she had arrived at his house, silent and solemn, climbing out of the car with Carl fussing behind her and Rhian rushing at her, full of questions and sympathy.

Rhian had drawn back tactfully, seeing Ginny's expression. For now, at least, she obviously had no intention of telling a dramatic story for everyone to enjoy.

'I think she's in shock,' Rhian whispered to Leo as she ushered him to help with the bags.

'So…'

Leo dumped her bags on the bed and waited. Obviously Ginny didn't want to talk, but Leo was anxious to know whether what had happened was the work of the Stealer, and he wanted to tell her about Bos and what had taken place at St David's.

'Was it… you know… was it something to do with him?'

'Of course it was. You know it was.' Ginny sat down beside the bags and pushed her hair back behind her ear, glancing out of the window at the garden and then at the ceiling, as though avoiding looking at Leo.

She looked different Leo thought, pinched and serious, not herself at all.

'You okay?' he asked.

She nodded.

Rhian called from down the stairs. 'You two!' she shouted. 'C'mon now. There's sandwiches and bara brith, and then we have to get going, and there's no more food till late tonight, so come and get as much inside you as you can.'

Leo knew the plan for the evening from his experience of many previous years, and Ginny was catching up fast as this was her third pantomime visit. First, there would be an ordinary tea – there always was on a first night, then they would travel down to the Little Theatre, where Rhian and Carl would disappear backstage with the rest of the company, and Leo and Ginny would hang about in the foyer until the audience started arriving, and then find their seats. After the performance, they would all, the entire cast and friends and families, head out to supper at Romano's Italian restaurant in Tenby. It was always a very jolly occasion, but looking at Ginny, Leo felt he would be surprised if anything made her feel jolly this evening.

She shrugged.

'Best go down,' she said.

'What's all this quiet mysterious stuff about?' Leo found himself asking. 'It's not like you to sulk.'

'I'm not sulking,' Ginny said. But she said it as if she didn't care whether he believed her or not.

'Well, you look like you are,' Leo answered, feeling irritated. 'There's things we need to talk about, and there's things I need to know.'

Ginny put her head in her hands as though she might burst into tears. Leo sat beside her. He felt that he would like to put his arm round her, comfort her, but she seemed prickly and distant and she might shove him away. So, he sat and waited.

‘'Okay,’ Ginny said slowly, raising her head. ‘Where's the brooch?’

Leo patted his pocket.

‘Gido told me to keep it on me,’ he said. ‘Why?’

For the first time, Ginny looked straight at him, and her expression was a mixture of amazement and disbelief.

‘So, you didn't give it to him in exchange for me?’ she asked.

‘No!’ Leo answered. ‘He sent Bos for it. But that was yesterday, after you'd been found. Look, I still have it.’

He took it from his pocket and showed it to her.

‘Thank goodness,’ Ginny almost smiled in her relief. ‘I thought maybe you'd given it to him. He said I would be his prisoner until he got the brooch, so I thought you must have given it to him.’

‘As if I would!’ Leo protested. ‘I'd have found you and rescued you, somehow. Where did he keep you?’

‘Somewhere in the castle,’ Ginny said. ‘It was all my fault. I followed him. Stupid, stupid thing to do, but I wanted to see where his den was so I could tell you.’

‘Is that where you went the night before?’ Leo asked.

She nodded.

‘I told my mum I'd been to see the Christmas lights both times. She was cross and said I should've told her.’

‘And was that where his den was?’

‘I don't know,’ Ginny shook her head. ‘I think he was only there to see whether I had the brooch. But then, he said he knew I didn't, so he would keep me till he got it.’

She paused.

'I was really, really, scared,' she said in a small voice.

'But you escaped!' Leo said. 'How did you do that?'

'I don't know,' Ginny shook her head. Unless the Keepers did it. Gido said they would try to tamper with time, to get me out, but I was asleep and...'

'Gido was there?' Leo asked in surprise.

'Not actually there,' Ginny said. 'In a dream, while I slept. I seemed to do a lot of sleeping. The Stealer has this way of singing that just made me go funny, and I couldn't keep awake. I'm so relieved you didn't give him the brooch. You don't know what he would be able to do if he got hold of it.'

'I can guess,' Leo said. 'Otherwise, Gido wouldn't keep going on about keeping it out of his hands. Tell me what happened, about the bat and everything...'

She shook her head.

'Later, maybe,' she said.

Rhian's voice calling them came up the stairs again. Ginny got up and went ahead of him. At the foot of the stairs, she spoke quietly, almost under her breath, but he heard her and it made him stop in his tracks.

'He knows you've still got it,' she said. 'I don't think he believed for a second that you'd thrown it away. And he won't stop coming after us until he gets it. I wouldn't like to guess how angry he was when he found me gone.'

The thought was an extremely uncomfortable one. Leo knew there was no way that he could pretend to know how to stop the Stealer. He could only reassure her with the small crumb of comfort that Gido had offered.

'There's a plan,' he said. 'Gido told me they have a plan. So, they're going to help us; that's for sure. Try not to worry.'

Ginny nodded. She still looked pale and tired and serious, and Leo realised she was still suffering from the shock of the experience.

Rhian was in a great mood at the tea table, laughing and chatting to Carl, excited about the coming performance. But somehow, the atmosphere changed when Ginny sat down, although Rhian tried her best to cheer her up.

'You wait till you see some of the dancing!' she said to her as she passed the sandwiches. 'Next year, you should join in. You're a good little dancer and you'll be old enough to get a part.'

'Thank you,' Ginny said politely, picking at the food, but she didn't really brighten up. She looked confused, and suddenly her eyes filled with tears, as though she was about to weep.

'You're still upset,' Rhian said hurriedly. 'You've had a very nasty shock. Try to put it behind you and enjoy the pantomime. It's going to be great fun.'

'Hey,' Carl said to his daughter, in his kindly way, 'come on; cheer up. Let's go out and have a good time. Think of how lucky you were that we found you before you got hypothermia! You'll start to feel better soon, you'll see. I'll bet we catch you laughing before the night's out!'

Ginny gave him a watery smile. Leo hoped he was right.

As far as Rhian and Carl were concerned, the worst that had happened was that Ginny had passed out after a bat landed on her face, and she had lain out in the cold all night. Only he knew that she had been a prisoner of the Stealer, and guessed what a terrifying experience it must have been.

When they arrived at the theatre, Carl took Leo briefly on one side before going backstage.

'I want you to watch her, make sure she's all right,' he said. 'If she gets upset or... well, or anything..., come and get me.'

'Okay,' Leo agreed. 'But I'm sure she'll be fine.'

He hoped he was right. They sat in the foyer together watching people arrive.

'Can you tell me about what happened?' Leo asked eventually. 'Just say yes or no to my questions, if you don't want to talk about it. What did the bat have to do with it? Was that something to do with the Stealer?'

She nodded.

'He was the bat,' she said, and then, as if she had decided that telling him was better than remaining silent, she began talking. Between sentences, she hesitated, choosing her words carefully.

'I fainted when the bat hit me. I came round in a building, more than likely in Castle Green, the ruin inside the castle walls. Just me, with him. I was terrified; hands tied, and a blindfold on, and he was gloating and laughing at me.'

'Oh, no,' Leo groaned. 'How terrifying! How awful! I don't know what to say. No wonder you don't want to talk about it.'

Ginny sniffed, pulled a bunch of tissues from her pocket and wiped her eyes and nose.

'I've still got a rotten cold,' she said. 'Anyway, he told me some stuff; stuff about Gido and Maria that I didn't want to hear, and how the brooch would make him so powerful and everything.'

She paused and gritted her teeth.

'I'd been in trouble the day before, at school, for answering back, so I was really careful not to do it again. Especially with him! I don't know how I didn't shout back at him, or make a big argument. I just kept thinking about how it would make things worse.'

'What did he tell you about Gido and Maria?' Leo was curious.

'That they were trapped like he was,' Ginny answered. 'That they were using us for their own purpose; things like that.'

Leo thought for a moment. He remembered Manawl's question, when they had seen him in the café at Narberth, just as he was leaving. 'Have you figured out why they want your help so much?' he had asked.

'It's possible there's things we don't know,' he said.

'Don't tell me you believe him?' Ginny said sharply. 'I trust the Keepers and I don't trust him. They got me out; okay?'

'What else did he say?' Leo asked.

Another long pause followed.

'Not a lot,' Ginny said. 'When I didn't answer him, I think he just sent me back to sleep and went away. Probably, he went to talk to that horrible boy, and get him to find you and the brooch.'

She looked down at her feet. She was wearing new shoes, and she looked as though she was admiring them, but Leo knew she was holding back the fear that returned when she talked about what she had gone through.

'Right,' he said. 'Let's forget it for now. No-one can get at us here. We're going to be surrounded by people all evening, and we're going to see a brilliant show. I think we can relax for a short while, at least. Maybe, if the Keepers rescued you, they're going to come through and help us. There must be a worm-hole coming up, or they wouldn't be able to do that.

She stopped and looked at her feet again.

'What?' Leo asked.

Ginny sighed.

'I don't want to keep remembering it. I wish it would go away and I could forget it. When I woke up in the morning, there were people all round me, going on about the bat on my face. They'd taken it off by then, but they showed it to me. I didn't want to look at it, but they thought they were being kind by showing me it was dead and not dangerous or anything. It was just a dead bat, but it was him when it landed on my face. I know it was.'

'It must have been horrible,' Leo said, feeling guilty about the larking about at the bus stop that morning. 'A bat! I can't imagine what that felt like.'

'Just be glad you'll probably never know,' Ginny said. 'So, with me lying there in the long grass and bushes, when they found me, they thought I'd been there, in the same place, all night, right where I'd fainted. I didn't say anything about what really happened. No point.'

'No,' Leo agreed. 'I'm just so glad I was able to tell Bos where to get off, when he tried to tell me you were a prisoner. You should've seen his face! Talk about shocked. He really thought you were still the Stealer's hostage …'

Leo stopped mid-sentence as Ginny lifted her head to look at him and he saw a look of such horror pass over her face that he turned to see who was behind him.

It was Bos. Leo leapt to his feet. Whether Bos had been about to mount an attack, or simply creep up on him and take him by surprise, was irrelevant. He was there and he should not have been. Leo was outraged.

'What d'you think you're doing here?' he asked, thrusting his chin at Bos, but careful to keep his voice low because of other people around. 'This is a first night. It's invitations only, if you don't mind!'

Bos didn't answer. He looked straight past Leo, and glared at Ginny with such an unfriendly and unpleasant expression that Leo wanted to thump him, there and then.

'Did you hear me?' Leo insisted. 'It's tickets only, for people who've been invited.'

'Get lost,' Bos sneered, turning his eyes to Leo as though reluctant to give him any attention. 'Yer fink yer know it all, don't yer? Well, yer don't. Because I'm'ere wiv Mr Brown, the teacher from my school, and'e's definitely invited. See. There'e is.'

He pointed to a man with a dark beard and spectacles, wearing a corduroy jacket; he was bearing down on them, with a friendly smile. Leo stepped back in shock and confusion. Up until that moment, Ginny had been sitting glowering at Bos, but, when she saw Mr Brown, she rose from her seat.

Leo couldn't read her face, but she looked sideways at him and gestured with a jerk of her head in the opposite direction, as though she thought they should move away. Mr Brown smiled at them pleasantly. His spectacles were tinted so that his eyes were difficult to see, but Leo felt sure that Ginny had sensed who the 'teacher' really was.

'These are friends of yours, are they?' he asked Bos. 'Great! I like to see young people interested in local theatre productions. Boris tells me he's always wanted to see a live pantomime and never been able to go to one, so I offered to bring him with me. I teach drama at his school.'

If it was the Stealer, he was certainly doing a professional act.

Everything about him was very much like a teacher, but Leo remembered the first time he had encountered a Stealer, when he was the jailer of the Keepers at the standing stones, and he had looked and sounded like a perfectly normal business man. Maybe this was the Stealer, maybe it wasn't. But, either way, Bos shouldn't be here, and it was all very suspicious.

Ginny was hovering, looking as though she might suddenly run from the building, but Leo decided the best way to handle the surprise intrusion was to act as normally as possible. He would make small-talk with the Stealer. The thought made him feel a thrill, as though, by leading the Stealer to believe in him as Bos's teacher, Leo might somehow outwit him.

'We come every year,' Leo said. 'It'll be a great show.'

Ginny looked startled and stared at Leo. He turned and looked at Bos.

'By the way, you never told me what school you're going to now,' he said.

He looked back at Mr Brown.

'Bos used to come to our school,' he said, by way of explanation.

'It's in'Averfordwest,' Bos replied. But he looked at the man as though he wasn't sure it was the right answer.

It was obvious that Bos was as afraid of the Stealer as he had been when Leo had last seen them together.

'Has it got a good drama department?' Leo asked Mr Brown.

'Oh, excellent,' smiled the pretend teacher. 'We put on a good show every year, and we have great facilities.'

Leo was beginning to think small-talk was not such a good idea. He was running out of ideas to keep the conversation going. It would soon be time for the pantomime to start, and Leo had no idea what the Stealer had in mind. People were now arriving in numbers, and the foyer was filling up rapidly. Amongst the throng, Leo spotted a familiar face. It was a moment of what he felt to be supreme good luck.

'Oh, look,' he cried. 'There's my teacher!'

With a broad smile, which he hoped looked sociable but came from relief, Leo called across to where he stood.

'Mr Evans! Come and meet Mr Brown, from Bos's new school.'

Mr Evans detached himself from the group of people around him and walked across.

He weighed up Mr Brown and Bos.

'Hello Boris,' he said.

Bos shuffled his feet and looked glum. He glanced up again at the man beside him, as if not sure what response to make.

'I hope you're doing better at your new school than you did with us,' Mr Evans said. 'Though, unless you have learned that work is necessary to improve your mind, I doubt it.'

'All school's are the same,' Bos mumbled.

'But not the one where this man teaches,' Mr Evans said.

Then, with a curt nod at Mr Brown, as though he knew him and he was a deadly enemy, he turned and spoke quietly, so that, although the others could hear his words, they were obviously meant for Leo and Ginny.

'Mr Brown used to be a teacher,' he said. 'He was dismissed from the profession some years ago. So I doubt he actually teaches Bos anything, other than a little thieving, perhaps.'

Then he returned his level gaze to Mr Brown and said, 'I'm

sure you have no objection to me explaining that small detail to these young friends of mine. I'm not sure what you are doing here, Brown, and I hope it is simply to watch a good show. But it is wrong of you to masquerade as a member of my trusted profession, since no-one has trusted you since you went to prison. Now you are returned to the outside world, I hope you may find some other type of employment that suits you. But don't call yourself a teacher. That is something you are not. And never will be again.'

It seemed, in the moment following his accusation, that everything went suddenly cold. Leo even looked up to see whether the doors had somehow swung wide open and let in the blast of cold air from outside. Both he and Ginny were stunned by Mr Evans's pronouncement and not sure what to make of it. It seemed that the man was actually a real Mr Brown, but was one of the Stealer's victims, through whom the Stealer could work his will.

Mr Brown took a handkerchief from his pocket, removed his glasses, and began to polish them, all the time staring directly at Mr Evans.

Leo could hardly stop himself grabbing Mr Evans's arm and shouting, 'Don't let him look at you!'

But, apparently, Mr Evans was quite capable of looking after himself. He turned and smiled at Leo, completely ignoring the glaring eyes.

'I'm looking forward to the panto, Leo. I've brought my sister, and her son, who is the same age as you. Would you like to come and meet them?'

'Thanks,' Leo said. 'I think we would. This is my stepsister, Ginny. She doesn't come to our school. She lives in Cardigan…'

'What a coincidence!' Mr Evans smiled in surprise. 'So does

my sister! Do come and join us.'

'Yes, thank you,' Ginny replied. 'That would be nice.'

They followed him across the foyer, Leo grateful and relieved and Ginny thinking that, although Mr Evans was a bit eccentric, there was something kind about him, and she felt safer with him than on their own.

They left Mr Brown and Bos standing looking after them, and before they reached Mr Evans's family, Mr Evans said very softly, 'That is a very dangerous man, and I would not like to think of either of you being anywhere near him. If he pesters you, let me know.'

'What did he do?' Leo whispered.

'What didn't he do,' murmured Mr Evans. 'Fraud, embezzlement, drug-running… want some more?'

'No, no,' Leo said, anxiously looking at Ginny, to see how she was taking it. Ginny seemed to have found her old spirit and was listening to Mr Evans' words with the same interest as Leo.

'How long was he in prison?' she asked.

'In and out for years,' Mr Evans said. 'But he has not been teaching for at least ten years. I thought he was still inside, to be honest.'

Before they could think what to do or say next, a woman appeared from the auditorium, ringing a bell to tell people there were only three minutes before they should take their seats for the performance. Mr Evans briefly introduced the two children to his sister and her son, Jack; and Leo told them about Rhian and Carl's part in the production. Both children liked Jack immediately. Ginny recognised him as one of the older boys she saw around her school, who was good at sports, and Leo saw a cheerful, intelligent face that he would be happy to get to know better.

'Right,' Mr Evans said. 'Introductions over, let's go in and get our seats.'

'I wonder if...' Leo began. He stopped, not knowing how to say what was on his mind.

What he was hoping was that Mr Evans might, if given a little information, become an ally in holding off the Stealer and Bos. It was a risky plan, but he trusted Mr Evans and thought it might work.

'Spit it out, Leo,' Mr Evans said. 'Something's troubling you?'

'Ginny and I found a rare Roman coin at Cilgerran Castle,' Leo began, speaking so quietly that, with all the noise around them, no-one, other than Mr Evans and Ginny, heard. He desperately hoped that Ginny would understand what he was trying to do and would back him up. 'And Bos thinks it's worth loads of money,' he continued. 'He keeps trying to get it off me. Do you think he might have told that man about it?'

'He was at the castle, when we found it,' Ginny broke in. 'He even attacked Leo with a baseball bat for it.' She knew exactly what Leo was doing, and if it meant having someone else to look after them, so much the better.

They were now standing in the queue that had formed. Bos and Mr Brown were some way behind them, and Leo was keeping an eye on the distance between them.

'Do you have it with you?' Mr Evans enquired.

Leo nodded.

'I thought it would be safer than leaving it somewhere, till we get it valued, you know?'

'May I see it,' Mr Evans whispered.

Leo looked at Ginny. To Leo's surprise, she nodded.

'Okay,' he murmured.

He slid his hand into his pocket and surreptitiously placed what looked like a tin lid into Mr Evans waiting hand. The movement was so swift and silent that no-one saw it change hands.

Mr Evans looked down at it doubtfully.

'It doesn't look valuable,' he started to say, but then, as he turned it, hidden in his hand, he looked up in surprise. 'But it feels extraordinary. Good heavens! I think it may be something very rare. Not Roman, I think, but Celtic, possibly.'

He passed it back to Leo with the same quick hand movement that he received it.

'You are possibly right about its value, and if your friend Boris…'

'He's not my friend,' Leo interrupted, slipping the brooch back into his pocket and wondering how many more times he was going to have to deny friendship with his enemy.

'No, no, of course he isn't; it was a figure of speech,' Mr Evans said. 'But, nonetheless, if he knows about it, he may well have joined forces with a crook like Brown to relieve you of it.'

'We're not sure how to get away from them,' Ginny said.

'Trust me,' Mr Evans said. 'Whilst we are here this evening, I will be alongside you all the time. If they make any move towards you, I will intercept their progress. But you must get this to a museum, for a thorough inspection and valuation, as soon as possible.'

'We will,' Leo answered, crossing his fingers behind his back.

They took their seats. Ginny made sure she sat right next to

Mr Evans, with Leo on her other side. She felt shaky about the Stealer's presence and was impressed with the fact that Mr Evans had felt something when he had touched the brooch.

Mr Hallet, the man whose metal detector had discovered the treasure, had examined it closely, and so had Izzy, her aunt, but neither had commented on the strange feel of the brooch. The fact that it could look like rubbish and yet feel like a precious artefact had been something only she and Leo had discovered until now. Within moments of them taking their seats, the lights went down and the theatre was plunged into darkness as the pantomime began.

First, the opening music changed from a loud cheerful rhythm to a slower, sadder tune. Then the curtains opened. The set was a kitchen with a huge fireplace, and Cinders, in her ragged clothes, was on her knees beside it, with a scrubbing brush. As the sad music died away she could be heard crying. Then, Buttons entered, smiling, playing the traditional role of cheering her up and making the audience laugh.

Ginny was trying to watch, but when the lights had gone down, the fear and panic that she had felt as the Stealer's prisoner had returned and gripped her. She struggled with it, hoping it would go away, but it didn't. It got worse. She felt that she couldn't breathe and was choking. She began to cough, trying to catch gulps of air.

Mr Evans, who had noticed that Ginny had a cold was sympathetic.

'You need a glass of water,' he murmured.

Then he leaned across to Leo and said, 'Take Ginny to the bar and get her a glass of water.'

Leo looked taken aback. He had seen Ginny was gasping, as though she was having an asthma attack, or something like one, but he didn't want to risk leaving their seats, in case they were followed by unwelcome company.

Mr Evans knew what he was thinking.

'Don't worry,' he said. 'Look, they're down there.'

He pointed to the two heads, some ten rows ahead.

'They're nearer the front than we are. Leave through the rear door, and if they make any move to follow, I'll be on my feet like a jack-rabbit to stop them.'

Leo hesitated. Ginny continued gasping and wheezing and coughing.

'I'm serious,' Mr Evans said. 'She isn't well. Take her to the Green Room, where your parents are, if she doesn't feel she can come back in. But, go. There is nothing to fear.'

They crept from their seats, Ginny holding a tissue to her mouth, to try to stop the explosive noises she was making, and they made their way to the rear entrance. In less than a minute, they were standing at the bar, where a barman gave her a glass of water, and after she had sipped at it and started to improve, he suggested that she go outside and take a breath of air, before going back in.

The gulping and coughing died down and, outside, on the car park at the back of the theatre, Ginny began to breathe properly again.

'Where do we go now?' Leo asked.

Ginny shrugged.

'We could go and sit in the Green Room with Rhian and Carl,' Leo said.

'I could, you mean,' Ginny said. She was feeling better, filling her lungs with fresh, cold air. 'You shouldn't miss it because of me.'

'I don't like the idea of us being in separate places,' Leo said.

They stood undecided for a few minutes.

Then Ginny said, with a note of sarcasm.

'P'raps the brooch knows where we should be!'

The brooch immediately moved in Leo's pocket. It was not a light twitch, which he was used to, but a strong thrust, like a bird intent on release. He looked at Ginny in disbelief. All the months he had held onto it, and it had never once moved on command, as if it had heard itself called upon. It occurred to him again that it was only when they were together that anything really interesting happened to it. Ginny obviously thought the same.

'Maybe, it only works when we're together,' she said. 'It didn't do anything for me, when I was on my own, and I first found it, did it?'

He withdrew it gently and looked at it. Ginny peered over his shoulder.

'Look,' she whispered. 'It's changing!'

It was transforming, even as they watched it, into the lustrous piece of jewellery that had once graced Manawl's cloak. Electric flashes passed across the surface, exactly as they had seen before.

'It's hardly done anything since the café in Narberth,' Leo said, reminding Ginny of the time they were faced with two Stealers. 'Honestly, for months, it wasn't even warm or anything. It's only in the last few days that it's started to be interesting again, at all. I'd begun to think it wasn't actually magic any more.'

'It's magic, all right,' Ginny commented. 'See, it's writing again, with the flashes. It's making words.'

Leo followed her finger as it traced the electric flashes that were illuminating the surface of the brooch, but, as far as he could see, there were no words, though he could make out shapes, like geometric figures. Ginny, however, was definitely seeing words, and she began to mouth them, silently at first, and then in a kind of humming murmur.

Leo got goose pimples. For a moment, he was tempted to drop the brooch and simply run for it. It was so eerie, standing outside in the dark, holding the flashing brooch, with Ginny reading a song from it, in what sounded like a foreign tongue. Was it ancient Welsh again? He couldn't understand it at all, but he hoped she knew what she was doing.

Looking at the flashes, he tried to concentrate on what he could see himself, and did not attempt to understand Ginny. There were three distinct lines of light, and they kept assembling in slightly different configurations. First, they were a triangle. Then, the three lines became one and turned into a screw shape, like a close-linked spiral, and, finally, into an arrow that flashed like an instruction on a computer. The first two shapes were no clue at all to Leo, but the arrow made him think that possibly it was pointing in a direction in which he and Ginny should be heading.

'Look,' he said, interrupting her funny chanting sounds. 'An arrow pointing up the hill towards the shops.'

She nodded.

'Great,' she said. 'It's not pointing to the shops! We did it! Close your eyes! Now!'

'What?' Leo drew back.

'Close your eyes, unless you want to be sick! I did it! We caught a worm-hole! We're going travelling. Can't you feel it?'

Chapter 6

The Truth at Last

There was a wooziness creeping into Leo's vision, and, around the car park, the trees blown by a fierce wind were throwing giant shadows, like great reaching arms.

'Don't be stupid...' Leo began, but his breath ran out and he heard Ginny calling.

'Don't be so bad-tempered! Close your eyes, remember the observATORY...,' she shouted and then she was gone, in a great blast of noise and wind, Leo was whizzing down a narrow road, with no control over his speed, nor any idea how he was being carried along, and he shut his eyes as tight as he was able, because it suddenly came back to him in a flash how horrible it had been when they had travelled into Dreamworld before, with eyes open, and Ginny had thrown up all over the place, and he had only just managed not to do the same.

This time it was like flying, but without height, so there was no sensation of landing, as such, when he arrived. He was just suddenly standing somewhere else. Carefully, cautiously, he opened one eye at a time. He felt queasy, but not sick. Ginny had beaten him to it and was sitting waiting for him. The brooch had fallen from his hands and was lying on the ground at their feet, in its other shape, the shape it had taken on the previous occasion they had ventured into Dreamworld.

It was a large, brown, leather-bound book, with gold lettering on the front, declaring it to be the Defnydd Hud, the Materia Magica, or book of spells created by the greatest magician before Merlin, Manawydan, son of Llyr, known to many as Manawl.

They were in a theatre. Not far from where they landed, a performance was taking place that seemed to be almost a mirror image of the pantomime they had been about to watch in the real world. There was an audience, who were evidently enjoying it, and waves of laughter and applause came across to where the two of them had landed, at the back, by one of the entrances.

'That's incredible,' Leo said, looking at the show. 'Even my mum's costumes!'

'Not really,' Ginny said. 'I should think Dreamworld is the place where pantomimes come from, and it has to be where Rhian gets her ideas for dresses!'

'Yeah, maybe' Leo chuckled.

He couldn't be bothered trying to work it out. He felt a bit light-headed, easy in himself, as though he didn't have a care in the world. He couldn't remember at first why they were there and what was going on; it almost felt like a dream. He saw the Grolchen, away across in the ranks of seats, and waved to him. The Grolchen registered them and called happily, 'Mic, mic.'

But, for now, he was enjoying the show and didn't approach them. Ginny watched, somehow disappointed that the Grolchen hadn't rushed up to them, delighted to see them.

'I've realised, since he talked to me, that we've never asked any questions,' she said. 'We've just rushed about doing…'

'Okay, okay,' Leo said, holding up a hand. 'I know what you mean and I've felt the same sometimes. It's like we've got dragged into their fight, and we don't get real answers from them about anything. But I think we're going to find out what it's all about, soon enough.'

'The Stealer told me they're trapped – just like him,' Ginny said.

'They were trapped, when we first met them,' Leo said. 'By him! Shall we ask the Defnydd Hud?'

Ginny looked wary.

'I wouldn't know what to ask,' she said.

Leo leaned down and opened the book, with no more idea than Ginny what to do next. Gido had shown them how to consult it, on the previous occasion they had used it, but that didn't mean it would work the same way this time. As he lifted the cover, a light breeze swirled across the book, lifting the pages, which fluttered over, one after another, for all the world as though an invisible hand were turning them, looking for a specific passage.

It stopped suddenly, and there, on the open page, in big gold curly letters, it said,

free me!

It made them jump. It was like a person speaking to them. Leo tried to turn the page, but no matter how many times he lifted it, the breeze simply blew it back, and 'FREE ME!' kept reappearing, and growing larger each time, until it appeared to take up the entire page.

They gave up.

'Spooky!' Ginny said. 'That's not a spell! I thought this was supposed to be a book of magic spells...'

'Well, that's what it is!' Leo said. 'But I think it means it wants to be like this in our world.'

'Well, why doesn't it tell us how to do it?' Ginny shrugged. 'It must have a spell to tell us…'

'I don't think it does,' Leo said. 'I think we have to figure it out.

He looked up and saw Gido and Maria heading towards them.

'Maybe they'll help us,' he said.

Ginny turned and saw them and ran towards them.

'Are you recovered from your ordeal?' Gido asked Ginny kindly.

'Oh, thank you so much for rescuing me,' she said. 'I was scared half to death, but I think I'm all right now. How did you do it?'

'The one thing on your side was that you were caught in a place where time, in a sense, had stood still for centuries,' Gido said. 'We are not masters of time but we can do tricks with it, especially in such a place. So, we moved whilst he was gone, and tried to return you to your garden gate before you left. That failed, but we did at least rescue you from his clutches.'

'Thank you,' Ginny breathed. 'I'm really grateful.'

Leo interrupted.

'He told Ginny you were using us and you were just like him,' he said. 'We know he was lying, but there are things we don't understand…'

'We are a long way from being like him,' Gido replied. 'But I should be less than honest if I deny that we have kept some of the truth from you.'

'That's what Manawl was talking about,' Leo exclaimed. 'In the Pendaran café, when he asked me if I knew why you'd enlisted our help, I knew at the time he meant something by it, but I asked you and you avoided answering.'

There was a brief silence. Gido and Maria looked at each other.

'We have never put you in danger without doing our very best to stay alongside and prevent harm reaching you,' Gido said.

'Start from the beginning,' Leo said. 'So we know what's going on.'

'We were locked in the stone. That much was true,' Gido said, and glanced towards Maria as though for support. 'However, it was also true that Grolchen, with his knowledge of song-spells, may, in time, have rescued us, but it could have taken years and, in the meantime… anyway, can you imagine our joy and relief, when not one but two children could hear us and maybe help us to escape? We felt it was destiny.'

Gido pointed to the page of the Defnydd Hud, still open in Ginny's arms.

'That says it all,' he said. 'That is telling you that your quest is nearly fulfilled.'

'It wants to be a book in our dimension, doesn't it?' Ginny asked.

'To put back what disappeared at Gors Fawr?' Leo asked, suddenly sure that's what it meant.

Gido nodded.

'You took my advice, and you've been reading again, have you, Leo?' he asked.

'Procton says you got it wrong,' Leo answered.

Ginny looked at him in surprise. It was the first she had heard that Leo knew something she didn't.

'A book, from Mr Evans,' he explained. 'You remember the legend where the Masters thought they were sending their wisdom to the Otherworld, and sent Gido down the well with it?'

'Procton was right,' Gido said. 'Our calculations and motives were at fault. When I died, I came into Dreamworld, where we cannot hide from our mistakes, and before I could move to Annwn with a clear conscience, I took on two quests. One was to replace what I, and my fellow masters, stole from the world. The second was to get rid of the Dreamstealers.'

'You told us your job was just to stop them doing too much harm…' Ginny began.

'I did,' Gido said carefully. 'That was stretching the truth. We always wanted them to return to Neptune. When you two turned up, we knew it was a possibility, but if we had asked you…'

'So you're trapped here, until you've done both those things?' Ginny asked sharply. She was following Gido's every word, watching his face. He had taken her by surprise by admitting they had not been honest.

'Trapped by my conscience, not by any outer barrier,' Gido said, shaking his head sadly. 'And Maria, a close friend in my lifetime, made the choice to stay here and assist me. The Grolchen attached himself to us, as a dog might to a human being. So, we became known in Dreamworld as the Dreamkeepers, because, if nothing else, we did keep control of the worst that the Stealers could achieve.'

'But why didn't you just tell us you wanted to get rid of them?' Leo asked, feeling confused. 'It wouldn't have made any difference to us.'

'Wouldn't it?' Maria put in. 'Can you childer be sure of the differenting it would make? You to be knowin' we wanted'em gone – at your hands?'

‘Ah,’ Leo said. ‘You’re right.’

‘Would you have helped us willingly?’ Gido asked.

‘No! We’d have run a mile,’ Ginny answered.

‘She’s spot on there,’ Leo said. ‘So, I suppose it was best that we didn’t know. But one of them is still around.’

‘And he’s the cleverest,’ Ginny added. ‘He’s the one that was your jailer, and in the café, and he controls Bos…’

Gido grimaced.

‘We know,’ he said.

But Leo’s mind had moved on to the other information Gido had given them, about their other remaining task.

‘This stuff about putting back the knowledge you took. We can’t do that, with him hanging around. Why bother with that, anyway. You didn’t rob the world on purpose.’

‘What I did was unwise and cheated generations,’ Gido said.

‘Well, if it’s going to mean him coming after us all the time, I think we’d prefer not to do it.’ Leo muttered.

‘I hope you will reconsider,’ Gido said. ‘We were seeking the whereabouts of the brooch for aeons. When the Stealers got close to it, we desperately wanted it. The fact that you recognise the Stealers when they are near you was why we came for your help a second time. If he were to get his hands on it, the consequences would be appalling. We had to use your abilities.’

‘But, what you’re saying,’ Ginny said, astonished, ‘is that, if we hadn’t gone after the brooch, the Stealer would have left us alone, and never bothered us again, after the stones?’

There was a small silence.

‘I can only ask you the same question again. Would you have helped us?’ Gido asked.

'No,' Leo said promptly. 'We probably wouldn't!'

'Exactly,' Gido said.

'He is sitting in the theatre – waiting for us!' Ginny almost yelled it. 'We can't do anything about the brooch, until he's gone. Will you get rid of him for us?'

Gido ignored her and looked up at the sky. Then he began to speak very quickly, as though things were becoming more urgent.

'The Defnydd Hud, instead of moving from brooch to book and back again, must be made to stay in its true form, as the book it really is. Not here in Dreamworld, where it can do no good, but back in the real world, where it may be read and used.'

Leo laughed.

'Fat chance!' he said. 'It does as it pleases. You can't read it, because it turns its own pages!'

'There will be some who will learn how to use it.' Gido responded. 'If the time is right, which I believe is why we met you.'

As he spoke his voice began to break up, like a bad telephone line. Leo watched closely, to try to read his lips, but his face, too, had begun to fade around the edges.

'Oh, blow,' Leo heard Ginny's voice cry, angry at the interference. 'This always happens!'

He saw her stoop to pick up the book, which was lying on the ground, and he recognised the blast of hot wind that he knew was about to thrust him back into his own dimension, but some part of him refused to go.

'I'm fed up of this,' he shouted. 'Every time we come here, it's the same, just when things are getting interesting. And you haven't said yet whether you will deal with the Stealer…'

'The moon,' shouted Gido. 'The wormhole! Go with it! Don't resist, or you'll find yourself on the outer circle.'

But Leo was already resisting, and was determined not to get tipped out of Dreamworld before he was ready to go. He grasped at a chair, in which one of the rapidly disintegrating figures that had made up the audience had been sitting, and held it firmly.

'I'm not leaving till you tell us what to do next!' he yelled.

Then he focussed his eyes on a spot on the ground and tightened his grip as the blast of wind hit him hard, making him feel as though he was about to take off.

He spoke, like an incantation, over and over again, 'I'm staying here, I'm staying here, I'm staying here.'

And just for good measure, though not because he really believed the words would help, he repeated some of the words the Keepers had given to him and Ginny, in their first inter-dimensional travelling.

'Garloyg molp,' he yelled. 'and Weebly Sleem and Plom Gyolrag.'

'Leo,' Ginny called. 'Leo, where are you?'

Her voice came to him as though she was far away. Leo stopped himself from looking up, and kept his eyes on the small square of very green grass in front of him. He clung like a mad thing to the wooden strut of the chair, whilst the noisy, scorching wind, which brought with it chaos and soup-like darkness, travelled across and around him. He felt the wind dying and he reared his head. The green square had gone and so had the heat and the darkness.

In place of all the activity, in front of him were walls, which wavered and listed, along a length of tunnel, or corridor, that seemed to go on for ever and tilted at a crazy downward angle before his dizzy eyes. He tried to walk forward, but was taken with such nausea, he immediately stood still again. He was holding something, and, looking down, he realised that he held a bar, not unlike the one on the back of the chair he had been holding, but which now seemed somehow fixed to the billowing wall at his side.

He held on tight to it. It was the only thing that made him feel a little better, to keep still. His eyeballs hurt, his head stung all over and his stomach churned. He wished he had listened to Gido. As though the thought had conjured him, Gido's voice came echoing from somewhere. The sound was not unlike that of someone shouting into a bottle.

'Leo, for goodness sake, why didn't you listen, boy?' he called, and the sound set up an echo that rocked Leo's centre. 'The Outer Circle is the worst of all places to find yourself. Can you move?'

Leo tried to speak but the effort made him want to throw up. The corridor wound away before his eyes, seeming to change from gloom to garish yellow light and back again as it twisted and turned in its downward spiral. From somewhere came the sound of heavy slapping and gurgling, as though a thick fluid ran down a steep invisible slope.

'Mnmn...' he heard himself mutter, in an effort to reply to Gido.

A harsh smell of acrid smoke drifted past his nostrils, and was gone before he could identify its source. He felt panic rising. The place was ghastly, and if this was what Gido and the others had to go through, to come to help Ginny and himself from time to time, he was amazed that they had made the journey and succeeded in returning.

'We're going to attempt to come in to get you Leo,' Gido said.

'Keep your head down, just in case you get company.'

Company? Leo wondered what on earth Gido could mean. He couldn't move, speak or think without either breaking into a sweat, feeling sick, or woozy, or getting double vision, so he could hardly imagine this being a place where one might happen across someone taking a stroll. But he was wrong. No sooner had he dismissed the idea than he heard footsteps. The steps were assured and firm; they did not belong to someone who was feeling sick or out of kilter.

'So, we find you without power,' said a voice, and laughed.

Leo held his breath. He had a horrible feeling he knew who was standing beside him, and he wished he was somewhere else.

'We meet in territory where you may gain greatly,' the voice was soft and gentle, but Leo knew it held a threat. 'But only if you come with me.'

Leo kept his eyes down, riveted to the floor, which swung and swayed under his stare.

'You only have to look at me and all will be well. Think of the relief,' the voice continued.

From the corner of his eye, Leo saw the outline shape of the skeletal figure once seen before. There was no disguise this time; no comfortable human figure cloaked the Dreamstealer's ghastly appearance.

'You don't want to stay there, holding on to the wall, cowering like an infant in fear of falling over, do you?' the Dreamstealer continued. 'I will take you to somewhere where you will feel quite recovered, and, then, we can talk about what you can do for me.'

What Leo wanted to say was, 'Over my dead body,' but the

effort to say it made it seem like it could actually happen, and all that came out was a strangled, 'Grrnnnnn.'

'Come along,' the Stealer cackled. 'You can't really be enjoying what's happening. And what is there to lose?'

Leo turned a fraction, and caught the smell of the Stealer, and it seemed to burn his nostrils. He felt pity and horror mingled. His stomach was turning horrible somersaults, and he wondered how long he could hold out for Gido's promised help to arrive, and whether, before he did, he would have looked into the eyes of the Stealer and accepted his invitation to be rescued.

He clung on. Time stood still. It seemed that days passed as he held on to the small bar, which kept him upright in the corridor of the Outer Circle. The Stealer hung around him, teasing and whispering, like a jackal waiting for his prey to expire so that he could leap and take swift advantage.

'I can make it all go away,' the Stealer murmured. 'I can make you feel right again, and all your dreams will come true. This place feels bad to you now, but if you say yes to me, it will feel very different. This is the timeless vault, the corridor of my power, and only I can guide you from here. We could share the brooch. The treasure Manawl left behind is locked within it. All his spells and all his hidden wealth...'

'Shut up,' Leo yelled, but it came out like 'Quaarb sclop!'

And the Stealer laughed at his misery, as though the joke were so huge he would never stop laughing, and Leo wanted to hit him, but could only stand shaking and quaking and wondering whether this was what it was like to have malaria or some terrible fever.

And as Leo retched and reeled and almost gave in to him, two things happened. The Stealer put out a hand and touched Leo on the shoulder. Then he drew back, alarmed, and began screaming at him,

'How can I touch you? Where is the brooch? Why do you not have the brooch? Where have you put it? Did you leave it in Dreamworld?'

And at that dangerous moment, Gido appeared out of nowhere, and, in one sudden strong movement, stretched out his firm hand and placed it on top of Leo's own hand, forcing him to release his grip on the bar.

Leo screamed as he floated, terrified, upwards, like a balloon without anchor, and Gido shouted 'Follow him… follow Grolchen… go… go…'

And the Grolchen dived between Leo's leg, crying 'Mic, mic, mic…'

'Chase,' Gido shouted again. 'Chase… put one leg in front of the other, chase… he knows where he goes… get out before the space-tide.'

Leo did as Gido said, and put his foot forward to follow the Grolchen. He slipped and spun round in a wild full circle, and found himself running backwards at speed, something he had never done before and never wanted to do again.

Behind him, there was no sign of Gido, who must have made a hasty exit, but the Stealer, furious that Leo did not have the brooch and uncertain whether it was back in Dreamworld, hovered, wondering whether to follow Leo or go back.

Beyond him, Leo saw what it was that had been making the horrible gurgling sound. It looked like a mountain of mercury, slithering rapidly down the slope of the tunnel. The Stealer seemed unaware of it approaching. He stood screaming and shouting at

Leo, his awful skeletal frame jerking and jumping with anger and frustration. His eyes glowed red, like lamps lighting up the dark tunnel, trying to force Leo to look at him, and before he knew what was happening, the wall of heavy silver liquid hit him, rolled right over him, and enveloped him.

Leo ran on in terror, still watching. If the Stealer had been frightening, this 'space-tide', as Gido had called it, was terrifying. But he couldn't take his eyes from it. The Stealer had disappeared completely into it, but the tide, like the tide of the sea, drew back, before its next great wave forward, and, as it retreated, it sprayed out loose bones in all directions.

Whether it was the sudden knowledge that the Dreamstealer had gone forever, or whether it was simply fear, from somewhere, Leo found the will to turn his body forward towards the running Grolchen.

He ran in fear and horror of what he had seen, down what seemed like miles of tunnel, which kept moving and changing. He had never run so fast, nor with such disgusting discomfort, in his life. It seemed as though his legs alone were moving with the required action, the rest of him floated and spun above them like a sea-sick baby being carried by a strong wind.

Ahead of him, the Grolchen scampered and swivelled, seeming to straighten the curves in the tunnel as he went. Behind him, the slopping, gurgling noise of the space tide crept nearer. Occasionally, the Grolchen slowed down, to check over his shoulder that Leo was following, and then, reassured, returned swiftly to his original high speed.

Leo wanted to think about what was happening, but he couldn't. Where his mind had been, there seemed to be a blur of runny stuff, sloshing about in his head. But some corner of him remembered what he had seen, and he was sure that the Dream-stealer had been gathered in by the tide. If only he, too, was not going to suffer the same fate, maybe all would be well.

And then there was an enormous explosion, somewhere up ahead, and, with a gigantic bang that hurt his ears, Leo saw the Grolchen burst through what looked like an immense wall, leaving a small ragged gap in it, where he had broken through. Instantly, the gap began to close again, like a hole in a jumper, knitting itself back together. Leo looked at it in alarm. There was no way he would be able to fit through it, even if it didn't close any further.

'I can't stop,' Leo screamed, though what actually emerged was more like a squawked 'Gwhark hoynah glurple...' and he hit the wall at such speed that the racket accompanying his breakthrough was even greater and louder than that of the Grolchen.

Chapter 7

Rescue Attempts

Whilst Leo ran the gauntlet of the Stealer and the Outer Circle, Ginny had found herself back in the car park, at the very spot where she and Leo had been standing before the brooch had taken them into Dreamworld. The brooch had returned to its medallion-like shape. It was glowing red in Ginny's hand, and was warm to the touch, but it told her nothing.

Out of the corner of her eye, she thought she saw Leo nearby, but when she turned to look, he had gone. She looked around her, feeling the air chillier, compared to where she had just come from. She saw, some distance away, the theatre lights glittering in the darkness.

'Leo, where are you!' she groaned, looking round for him and wondering how long she was going to have to wait for him.

Was it possible, she wondered, that he had managed to stay behind, and, if he had done, what would that mean? Would he ever get back again? She told herself not to jump to conclusions. There had been times before when a moment or two had passed between them both returning.

She leaned on the stone wall at the perimeter of the car park. Her eyes were becoming accustomed to the dark, and again she caught sight of Leo, in mid-air, some twenty yards from where she stood. But the image of him had no solidity, and came and went again. It was worrying, and she began to feel more and more uncomfortable about him not arriving.

He was, it seemed, trying to get through, but somehow not achieving it. She wished she had someone to speak to, someone with whom she could share what had been happening. She had barely recovered from her ordeal of being taken by the Stealer, and now she trembled at the possibility that Leo was lost between dimensions. She thought of going back into the theatre, and remembered Bos and Mr Brown. Had they noticed that she and Leo had gone, she wondered now, or were they sitting watching the pantomime?

And then another thought occurred to her. How long had she and Leo been away? She looked at her watch, but couldn't read it in the dark. Maybe, a few moments had passed, or maybe, hours had gone by. She had no way of knowing, since on every occasion they had been carried through the dimensional tunnel, time had been different. She moved towards where there was a street lamp, under which she consulted her watch again. A mere ten minutes had passed since she and Leo had first walked into the auditorium and left by the rear door.

'Ginny,' a woman's voice called her name.

It made her jump and she turned, thinking she recognised it, but not daring to believe who it was. The voice came from between the parked cars. A woman in a parka with a big furry hood was walking towards her, with a small grey, dachshund-like dog on a lead.

'Mum!' Ginny cried, 'and Basil! What are you doing here?'

'Well, I'm supposed to be here to see the pantomime!' Sara said. 'Rhian and your father asked me if I would like to come, but Basil was misbehaving and made me late. Am I glad to see you!

Are you late, too, sweetheart?'

'No,' Ginny said, confused, but delighted to see her mother and even more pleased that she had brought Basil with her. 'I needed to get some fresh air. Got a bit... you know... claustro whatsit... in there...'

'Of course,' her mother sympathised. 'That bat has a lot to answer for!'

'What?'

'Of course, it couldn't help it. I don't mean that. Poor thing didn't know it was coming to its final rest on your nose, did it?'

'Er no...'

'I expect it was as shocked as you were...'

To Sara's surprise, Ginny was so glad to see her and hear her chatter, she interrupted what she was saying by suddenly hugging her warmly.

'Oh, thanks for coming, mum,' she said, and she meant it. 'I didn't know they'd invited you. They never said, and it's such a long way.'

Her mother shrugged.

'I think they only asked out of politeness, because you were coming. But I thought, why not? I never go to anything... so here I am. Shall we go in?'

'Only problem, mum,' Ginny stooped to stroke Basil and give him a cuddle. 'We can't take Basil in.'

'His fault I didn't get here in time,' her mother said, looking down at him disapprovingly. 'He wouldn't let me leave without him. Every time I opened the front door, he shot out in front of me. Then, I locked him in the kitchen, but when I started up the car and looked in the rear view mirror, he was running along behind me! How he got out, I've no idea. And what's got into him, I do not know! I know you're not supposed to take dogs into the theatre, but do you think he knows that? Or, even if he did, would he take any notice? Not a bit of it.'

'He'll have to wait in the car,' Ginny said. She continued to stroke the little animal, and noted the gleam in his sharp, button-like eyes that gazed back up at her. He had no intention of being left anywhere, she could tell. She wished Leo would return and tell her everything was okay.

'Maybe,' she said, thinking aloud. 'Maybe, we should wait to go in to the theatre until the interval. Leo came out with me and went for a walk, so I shouldn't leave till he's here, anyway.'

'And what do we do in the meantime?' Sara asked, surprised.

'We could give Basil a good walk, to tire him out, so he won't mind being left in the car,' Ginny said.

'That's very thoughtful,' Sara said, 'and a jolly good idea, because I have a feeling he isn't ready to settle down.'

They set off together, walking round the perimeter of the car park and along the back of the theatre. Basil began to pull on the lead at this point, determined, it seemed, to go his own way.

'Oh, let's go with him, as long as he doesn't want to go too far,' Sara laughed. 'He gets these ideas. Sometimes, I think he knows his way round places better than I do.'

They followed the straining Basil, and branched off down a path that ran along behind the buildings on the main street. Her mother chatted cheerfully, without a care in the world, while Ginny fretted, and wondered what had happened to Leo, and whether the Stealer was still in the theatre.

'Sometimes,' Sara said, as they walked, 'I think Basil has never really been right since Rolf died. He was like a big brother to him, as well as his best friend, and he taught Basil everything. I trained Rolf but Rolf trained Basil, that's for sure.'

Basil's ears pricked up.

'He was a lovely dog,' she continued. 'Brighter than many a human, as I've said more than once. And, wherever I've been, I've never seen another dog like Rolf anywhere, part Welsh collie, part Irish hound and part St Bernard, the vet reckoned he was – how's that for a rare combination? You don't see many like that around here!'

A dog barked, somewhere ahead of them, and the sound was like Rolf's bark, which they remembered so well, and all three froze where they were, shocked for a moment. Basil's nose went up, and Ginny and her mother stared. And out of the shadows, a large dog bounced towards them.

'Good grief!' Ginny's mother cried. 'It's so like... it can't be...!'

Leo's legs were slowing down and he was moving more gently along a path, which was solid under his feet. Around him, the buildings stood still when he looked at them, and it was night time. There were lights on here and there that made him feel safe, the sloshing in his head had gone and his mind had returned to tell him who he was. He knew he had re-entered the real world.

He laughed out loud with relief, though still uncertain where he was and what day of the week it was. He saw, in front of him, leading the way, a big black dog that reminded him of Rolf, Ginny's dog who had died, but which he knew, in reality, was the Grolchen.

Then, to his astonishment, he saw Ginny and her mother coming towards s him out of the darkness.

'There you are!' cried Ginny as though he really had just been round the corner for a walk. 'Thank goodness!'

Leo came to a stop, and stood open-mouthed in astonishment as he watched them approach. He was trying to work out how it could possibly be the same evening and the same place as before.

'Is that your dog?' Ginny's mother said, seeming to notice nothing odd about Leo suddenly appearing out of nowhere, and showing far more interest in the animal that had preceded him.

She gazed lovingly at the Grolchen, who, unable to come as himself, since he was a dream animal that did not exist in the real world, had emerged in the shape of Rolf, a form he had taken on a previous visit. It was apparent, too, that not only Ginny's mum, but also Basil, was fascinated by the Rolf look-alike, and he sniffed happily around him.

'Is that your dog?' Ginny's mum asked again.

'Er… no,' Leo said, while trying to decide how to explain the matter. 'I'm minding him for someone.'

'He's beautiful,' Ginny's mum sighed. 'And he's the spitting image of our dog that died. You might remember; we had a dog like this one, called Rolf.'

'Yes, I remember Rolf, 'Leo said, and anxious to change the subject, he asked, 'What are you two doing here, walking down the street in the dark?'

'We were giving Basil a walk. Mum was late,' Ginny said. 'We've missed the first half of the pantomime but we thought we could go in at the interval.'

'Good idea,' Leo agreed, still astonished that so little time had passed. If he had been asked, he would have said he'd been on the Outer Circle for at least a week.

'Will you be all right going back in there?' Sara asked Ginny.

'I think so,' Ginny answered. 'I know what to expect this time.'

Leo moved closer to Ginny, and, eyes shining, whispered in her ear.

'He's gone! I'm sure of it. We did it!'

Ginny's mouth dropped open. She stared at Leo in disbelief.

Ginny's mum couldn't take her eyes off the Rolf dog, and as she began to walk back towards the car park, with Basil on his lead, the Grolchen followed close to her, looking up at her as though he were indeed her devoted Rolf.

'Do you mean it? Truly, truly?' Ginny asked Leo, as they stood for a moment before following her mother.

'Unless he can put himself back together again,' Leo said. 'Caught by what Gido called the space-tide. It was incredible, awful. He just disintegrated right in front of me. I ran for my life, I can tell you. I thought it might get me, too! It would've done, if it hadn't been for our old friend there.' He nodded towards the Grolchen.

'D'you think that your friend would sell him?' Sara called to Leo. 'I'd love to have a Rolf again.'

'His name isn't Rolf,' Leo said quickly, as they went to join her. 'It's Grolchen, and no, his owner won't sell him. I'm sure of that.'

'That's a funny name, isn't it?' she said. 'Is it foreign? I've never heard it before.'

'Well, yes,' Leo said, crossing his fingers. 'His owners are foreign. They live in a country a long way away.'

'Maybe they would like me to mind him sometimes,' she sighed. 'Like you do?'

'Oh, er... it's, erm... possible, I suppose,' Leo said, not sure quite how to get out of the conversation.

'I'm not just an ordinary dog lover,' Sara continued. 'Ginny'll tell you. I'm a proper trainer. I can talk to them, and they like me ever such a lot, and they do everything I ask them – don't they, Ginny, don't they?'

Ginny had been following behind, doing a little dance of joy at the thought of the Dreamstealer having gone forever. Whatever else lay up ahead, this was the best news she could have hoped for. She was beaming from ear to ear and jumping up and down, when her mother turned to speak to her.

'Yes, yes,' Ginny answered happily. 'You are, without doubt, the best doggy person in the world.'

'Don't go over the top, dear,' her mother said. 'Are you all right?'

'All right! All right!' Ginny exclaimed. 'I'm so happy I could do cartwheels.'

Leo was laughing.

'Whatever's got into the two of you? You're like a pair of kiddies,' her mother said. 'We're only going to a pantomime.'

She gave them an odd look and decided to go back to the safe topic of dogs.

'Sometimes, I think animals understand me better than human beings do,' continued her mother. 'I'm never happier than when I've got a dog to talk to.'

Uncannily to Leo, the Grolchen was gazing up adoringly at

Ginny's mother, and seemed not only willing to be stroked but positively anxious to get near to her and enjoy her flattering words. She leaned down and cuddled him.

'Where will you leave him, when we go into the theatre?' she asked Leo. 'You can't just let him hang about outside, can you?'

Ginny sneaked a look at Leo's confused face and found herself giggling. She was used to her mother's eccentricities, particularly her over-the-top love of dogs, but she wondered how Leo would deal with it. He obviously had no idea what to do with the Rolf dog, who, having had the stroking he wanted, was now happily running around with Basil, and showing every sign of thoroughly enjoying himself. If her mother hadn't been there, perhaps Leo would simply have let the Grolchen run off, but he could hardly do that now, under Sara's watchful eye.

Ginny caught Leo's eye with a questioning look, unable to stop giggling.

Leo understood that he had to think of something fast.

'I might have to tie him up,' he said decisively to Ginny's mother. 'There are some posts at the front of the building.'

But by the time they had reached the car park, the sleet had now returned and was beginning to thicken, turning into full-blown snowflakes, and as Ginny's mother opened the back of the car and lifted Basil into his cosy bed, she said,

'They get on well enough, don't they? I'll tell you what. You can't leave him out in the snow, can you? Let him get in with Basil, and he can stay nice and warm. They'll curl up together, I expect.'

Before Leo had a chance to answer, Rolf jumped in beside Basil and settled down, after a brief look round, as though it was the nicest place in the world to find himself.

'I'm not sure whether he'll stay there for very long,' Leo said doubtfully.

'He won't have much choice,' Ginny's mum laughed as she banged the hatch-back shut. 'We won't be coming back until the end of the show. Right, let's get in there and see the second half at least. I've not come all this way just to stand in a car park all night.'

The first half was just coming to an end as they entered the theatre foyer. People were pouring out of the auditorium and into the bar area. A queue was forming at the ice-cream kiosk. Ginny was still grinning like a lunatic. Leo was in a kind of daze.

It was gradually dawning on him that, thanks to his stubborn resistance to following the worm-hole, he had, without actually doing anything, got rid of the Dreamstealer. His relief, mingled with the awesome thought that he and Ginny had achieved what the Keepers had been trying to do for centuries, made him feel elated and excited.

'There's Bos,' he said, as he saw his old enemy appearing from within the auditorium.

'But where is Mr Brown?' whispered Ginny.

'I doubt we'll see him here,' Leo replied. 'I expect, when he left Mr Brown's body, Mr Brown wondered what he was doing sitting next to a stink-bomb like Bos!'

They watched Bos, who looked about him as though he was searching for someone. When he caught Leo's eye, he turned away with a look of confusion, as though he wasn't sure what to do. Then, he appeared to make a decision and, pulling on his coat, he headed towards the outer doors. Leo was determined to face him, and knew that if he allowed Bos simply to walk away, he would regret it. Now, he could stand up to Bos on equal terms, with no fearsome figure lurking behind him. He walked quickly and stepped in front of him, blocking his way to the doors.

'Going home already?' he asked.

'What's it gorra do wi' you?' Bos replied, attempting to push past him.

'Oh, very friendly!' Leo said, standing his ground. 'Where's your teacher gone?'

'If you mus' know,'e thought it were a pile of rubbish and'e went'ome,' Bos said. 'Like I'm doin' now.'

'Oh, really?' Leo said, with some sarcasm. 'Well, I'll tell the cast, and I'm sure they'll be terribly upset.'

Bos snarled and continued to try to get round Leo to the door.

'He didn't stay long, then?' Leo said, and put himself between Bos and the exit.

Bos didn't answer and tried to push past.

'Did he wake up and realise he didn't want to be there?' Leo asked, unable to keep it to himself. 'That's because he's gone. Your puppet-master. Gone. Gone. Gone. Never to be seen again. No more pocket money. No more face painting...'

Bos stared but didn't respond and, with a final shove, thrust his way out of the building and into the snowy night. Leo was getting to him, there was no doubt about it.

Leo watched him leave and then turned to rejoin Ginny and Sara, just as Rhian and Carl headed towards them. Before they could start asking awkward questions about whether they had been enjoying the performance so far, Ginny jumped in by saying, 'Isn't it nice that mum's managed to make it?'

'Sara,' cried Rhian to Ginny's mum. 'How nice of you, to drive all this way. We weren't sure whether you would get here or not, especially when we heard the weather forecast. Come and let us get you a drink.'

She and Carl whisked her away to the bar, whilst the two children stood a little apart.

'Bos reckoned his teacher had gone home because he thought it was a load of rubbish,' Leo chuckled.

''But we know different,' Ginny said. 'Leo, I can't believe it. You know what this means. All three are gone and we have done something amazing. I never thought it would happen like that.'

'Nor me,' Leo said. 'Ask me if I'd do it again and I have to say, no. Like Gido said, sometimes it better not to know...'

The memory of the place caused a painful frown to cross his face.

'Believe me,' he added. 'It isn't somewhere you want to go, ever! I will never mess around again, when a worm-hole opens. I'll be straight through it and no hanging about! Anyway, he was there the whole time, almost as though he'd been waiting for me. And he was going on and on about sharing Manawl's treasure, and how he could save me. If it hadn't been for Gido and the Grolchen, I don't know what would have happened, once he knew I didn't have the brooch.'

'Do you think he followed us, when we went outside?' Ginny asked.

'I expect so,' Leo said. 'Even if Mr Evans stopped Mr Brown coming after us, he didn't know the Stealer was using Brown's body, did he? Bos looked pretty miffed, actually, didn't you think?'

'Yes, he did. But I shouldn't think a little thing like leaving Bos to get home on his own would bother a Stealer if he had other plans,' Ginny said. 'He wanted the brooch. I don't think he cared about anything else, and he never showed any kind of feelings for Bos, last time around.'

There was no time to say more, as Carl suddenly reappeared with ice-creams for them, and, before they knew it, the lady with the bell was going round, and everyone was being asked to return to the auditorium.

'Right,' Carl said, 'Rhian and I had better get backstage again. I'll make sure Sara finds her seat. I'm afraid she's nowhere near you two. We were lucky to get her a last minute ticket at all. We'll meet you out here at the end. Okay? Enjoy yourselves.'

With a brief wave of the hand, he disappeared into the crowd.

'That's lucky, about your mum's seat,' Leo said. 'No-one will notice we're not in there.'

'Er... someone will,' Ginny nodded towards Mr Evans, who was approaching them with a look of concern.

'You've missed the whole of the first half!' he said, 'and it's wonderful, a great show. Do congratulate your mother on her costumes, Leo, they're magnificent.'

'Thank you. I will,' Leo said.

'Brown left,' Mr Evans said quietly. 'Not so long after you. I followed, to see whether he was up to no good, but he simply got in his car and left. I'm not surprised. I never thought of him as a man who would enjoy a good pantomime, but I think your fears about his motive were perhaps mistaken. Do get that coin valued though, won't you?'

'Certainly will,' Leo said. 'Ginny's claustrophobic, so we're going back to the Green Room with mum and Carl.'

'What a shame,' Mr Evans said, shaking his head and looking at Ginny. 'Perhaps, another evening, you may feel better. I hope you get to see the whole show soon.'

With that, he joined his own party and they went into the auditorium.

'Phew,' Leo said. 'I've told more lies tonight than in my whole life. Do us a favour, will you? Go and ask your mum for the keys to the car. Tell her you need to put something in it. Your jumper, your scarf, anything... Quick.'

'Why?' Ginny asked.

'So we can get the Grolchen out, of course,' he hissed. 'It's not right for him to be trapped in there, and he might just decide to chew his way out, or something. Quick, now, before she goes in.'

Ginny ran across to her mother, who had joined the queue moving into the auditorium, and, pulling her thick scarf from round her neck, she wiped her hand across her forehead, and huffed and puffed a bit, as though she was sweating. Leo watched as she put out her hand for the keys, and Sara, looking slightly puzzled, passed them to her, before she disappeared in to watch the pantomime.

It took only seconds and Ginny returned triumphant.

'Mum says to hurry up and get into our seats before they close the doors,' she said.

'Well done! Come on,' Leo said, taking the keys.

'I wonder if Gido and Maria know the space-tide took him. I'm dying to tell them,' Ginny said.

'Maybe, we can send a message to them with Grolchen,' Leo

said. 'They didn't tell us how to go about this thing with the brooch, did they? I'm not sure whether they think we'll just find out by ourselves, or what. I don't mind missing the pantomime, but I don't fancy hanging around outside with the brooch again.'

Ginny pulled it from her pocket and held it out to him.

'Here,' she said. 'Take it. You know it spooks me. I don't know how I came to get hold of it. Maybe, if you'd kept it in your hands, you wouldn't have got lost in the Outer Circle.'

'And maybe, I would have got swept away...' Leo began.

'Stop it!' Ginny cried. 'Don't think about it. It's like when I was his prisoner. You can't keep going over it. It's finished.'

She gave little happy bounce as she passed over the brooch.

'It isn't doing anything,' she said. 'It's back to the old tin lid again.'

Leo took it from her hand and rolled it in his.

He wasn't sure what to do next, but one thing he knew. Outside in the car, the Grolchen might be straining to get home, and there was no knowing what he would get up to in order to release himself.

Outside, the snow had stopped again. A light powdering of white fringed the driveway to the car park, where they walked. It was cold and threatening to ice over, Ginny pulled her scarf back on and zipped up her coat. Leo dug his hands further into his pockets. The sky was black and starry, with a high moon, full and majestic, floating above them as they walked.

'Apart from letting the Grolchen go, I don't see what else we can do,' Ginny said, her breath curling in front of her as they walked quickly to keep warm.

'Neither do I,' Leo agreed, 'but we're not going to find out by sitting in there, watching Buttons telling jokes. The trouble is, we don't know what to expect. No-one seems to have any control over the brooch, so it isn't going to be easy, is it? It seems to switch on and off when it likes. Nothing I've tried has worked.'

He stopped suddenly and stood very still, looking into the gloom across the car park.

'Who are those people hanging round your car?' he asked quietly.

Ginny peered to where he pointed.

There were two people at the rear of the car, looking inside with interest.

'Maybe the dogs have been barking, or something,' she murmured.

They crept a little further forward, to gain a better view of what was going on, and crouched behind a parked vehicle, a sufficient distance away to keep themselves out of sight. They could hear the mumble of voices from where they were, and could make out that there was a man and a woman, and a fairly intense discussion was in progress.

'Can you hear what they're saying?' Leo mouthed to Ginny.

'I heard them mention 'the dog',' she whispered.

They watched as the couple came to the end of their discussion and, apparently in agreement, stood back from the car

Then the man raised his arm and, with a pointing finger, aimed at the hatch back door.

'I'll give it a try,' they heard him say. 'But I've no idea if it will do the trick.'

And then he uttered a string of incomprehensible words.

There was a brief flash on the lock of the car door, and the woman ran and tugged at it.

'No,' she said. 'Nothing doing.'

Leo was just about to suggest that they should go and look for some help, when Ginny took him completely by surprise by suddenly leaping out from their hiding place and heading straight towards the couple.

'What d'you think you're doing?' she yelled. 'Leave our car alone!'

So, Leo had no choice but to follow.

Chapter 8

Goodbye Grolchen

Leo did his best to catch up with Ginny, who ran, without a thought for her safety, towards her mother's car and her beloved Basil in the back of it.

'Ginny, please!' Leo called after her, in an effort to slow her down, but she appeared not to hear him.

'Get off,' she shouted, waving her arms angrily at the people round the car. 'Leave it alone!'

The couple turned to face the oncoming children, and Ginny came to a sudden halt and stared at them.

'Gido?' she gasped uncertainly. 'Maria?

Leo came up beside her and together they stood and stared at the elderly man and woman, who looked like anybody's nice grandparents. Both Leo and Ginny had seen Gido and Maria take these roles before, and recognised them, despite the fact they didn't look a lot like themselves.

Gone was Maria's wonky bun and funny little shoes and apron. Instead, she wore a smart brown coat and hat and warm winter boots. Beside her, Gido, instead of his frock coat and colourful waistcoat, was wearing a long warm overcoat and a woollen hat, from which wisps of his grey hair escaped. He stood, blowing on his freezing fingers, which only a moment ago had been aimed at the car, before replacing his gloves, and standing to stare at the sight of the children.

'Oh, there you are,' he said. 'We wondered how long you would be. We followed you back. Golly, you scared us to death, Leo!'

For a moment, it seemed from his serious expression that he was going to launch into a lecture, but his face suddenly broke into an enormous grin.

'You did it, young man!' he cried. 'You got rid of him!'

He and Maria clapped their hands and did a little capering dance, linking arms together and romping back and forth.

Leo and Ginny couldn't stop laughing.

'Isn't it brilliant?' Ginny asked when the laughter subsided.

Gido went to each of them, shaking their hands vigorously and patting their backs. Maria followed, doing the same.

'Brilliant is the word!' Gido said.

You'll never guess how it happened,' Leo began. 'There was this great woosh of silver stuff...'

'We know what happened. It was a high space-tide,' Gido said. 'I only just managed to dodge it. And you... why, I've never seen anyone run so fast!'

Before Leo could say how awful it had been, Gido rattled on.

'Amazing how like a sea-tide it is, isn't it? And it's even more dangerous. What you did is the talk of all Dreamworld. Can you imagine what it means? Good dreams can blossom, bad dreams will drop away. The infected humans will have no power to recharge their dreadful passions, and the influence of the Dreamstealers will become a forgotten page in history.'

He looked at them with real affection.

'You are both young heroes. All three of the dreaded zombies from the Cauldron disposed of, thanks to you. The world, as well as Dreamworld, is in your debt.'

'I feel a bit of a cheat, really,' Leo said. 'It happened by accident...'

'Or by the intervention of fate,' smiled Gido. 'What does it matter? You're not a cheat, and both of you have been so brave, so constant and so reliable. There is only one task remaining, and when that is finished, it will be a case of what can we do for you?'

All four were smiling broadly. There was a definite sense of celebration in the air.

'He was the worst of the lot,' Leo said, 'because he was the cleverest.'

'You're right there!' Maria said.

'He considered himself to be very clever,' Gido said, 'and more of an expert than he was, when it came to travelling out on the edge, simply because he did not feel the appalling discomfort that we do, and I suspect you may have done?'

Leo nodded, remembering for a sickening moment what it had been like.

'Horribly horrible,' he said.

'Because he did not feel the ill effects, he forgot that he should not linger there long,' Gido continued. 'There is a limited time one can spend in the Outer Circle without the tide drawing one to a point of polarity. The irresistible attraction of Neptune's backward space-tide drew him to his destiny. So, he was carried by nature's ebb and flow to Neptune, in the end, and Leo's stubborn refusal to do as he should have done, turned into a good deed.'

He turned and smiled at Leo.

'Does that make it worth the agony of the Outer Circle?'

'Er… well… yes, of course it does,' Leo laughed.

Ginny was jumping up and down, doing a little dance on the spot.

'I'm so happy,' she said. 'You don't know how it feels.'

'I think we do,' Gido nodded, 'but there is one more task, as you know, and though it should run smoothly now he is out of the way, it still needs careful planning and handling.'

Then, turning to more immediate matters, he reached out his hand.

'You wouldn't, by any chance, have a key to the car?' he asked. 'So we could let Grolchen out? He needs to come back with us.'

'But…' Ginny stopped before saying more.

They all turned to hear what she had to say.

'Now he's gone,' she said a little uncertainly. 'Once we've got the book back on earth, you will be going on to Annwn, won't you, to a beautiful place, where you can meet all your friends and have a lovely time.'

She looked from one to another, and they both nodded.

'Can't wait,' Maria smiled.

'But Grolchen will be left in Dreamworld on his own then, with no-one to love him and look after him.' Ginny finished.

'Grolchen will find a way of attaching himself to someone else, some other person with a quest…' Gido said.

'Why can't he stay here?' Ginny asked. 'Look.'

She pointed into the car, and they all looked inside, where Basil and Rolf the Grolchen lay curled together in a friendly, slightly steaming heap.

'He seems so happy,' she said.

'Look d'you have a key, or not?' Gido enquired. 'If you don't, then I shall just have to try the opening spell again. The trouble is, I had to reduce the power because of the other creature being in there. It wouldn't hurt the Grolchen, of course, but I wouldn't want to deafen the poor little dog.'

'You're not listening to me,' Ginny cried. 'I can't bear to think of him being all on his own.'

Gido stood looking at her, as if he was trying to work something out.

'Are you telling us you love the Grolchen?' he asked.

'Of course we do,' Leo interrupted. 'He's saved my life at least twice. He's a brilliant musician, and he's just loads of fun as well. Please. Ginny's right. Why should he stay lonely in Dreamworld, when he could be here, loved and looked after.'

Leo turned to Maria.

'Can we do it?' he asked.

'If they do love him, of course it can be done,' she said.

She pointed to the car.

'Let them out,' she said.

Leo held up the key.

'No worries,' he said. 'We were planning to let him out, as it happens. What're you going to do?'

'We'll offer him the choice,' Gido said. 'One of the rules of Dreamworld is that, if a creature is well enough loved on earth, he may, at some point, take form in the real world. It means he will be subject to the discomforts of carrying a real body and all its weaknesses. Compared to the life he would enjoy in Dreamworld, it has its difficulties, and is of limited length, as is all life on earth. But it's up to him.'

The moment Leo threw open the rear door, both animals jumped out, falling over each other to greet Ginny and Leo with such energy and enthusiasm that it looked as though they had been confined for days, though it was, in fact, less than half an hour.

'I don't think he'll want to go back to being the Grolchen,' Ginny said, stroking the Rolf look-alike, as he stood on his back legs, with his paws on her shoulders, wagging his tail. 'I think he'd like to stay being a Rolf!'

Gido spoke directly to the Grolchen.

'Are you coming back with us?' he asked. 'Do you wish to stay? You are loved here, so, if you wish, we will leave without you.'

If the Grolchen understood the words, so at the same time, it seemed, did Basil. Both dogs suddenly began scampering about, jumping excitedly and woofing with enthusiasm.

'See!' Ginny laughed. 'He's saying he wants to stay.'

'Well, well,' Maria said. 'He knows the laws of life. Maybe it will be for the best. I can't think of anyone in Dreamworld he showed a soft spot for like he does with you children.'

'And my mum…' Ginny added. 'She'll be so happy! He's really going to stay. Will he still be able to do all the amazing things he can do, like making music and…'

'Look,' Gido interrupted, pointing to the sky. 'We can't stand around here talking about the Grolchen all night. Time will tell what skills he might keep. There are things we really do need to discuss, and we could be making good use of the time we have here, to ensure that we guide you to freeing the brooch…'

'We must leave soon,' Maria said. She too was watching the

sky, and seemed to be taking notice of where the moon was, but also scanning right across the heavens, as though looking for something in particular.

'Indeed, we must,' Gido said. 'A moment, only a moment…'

He put his hand into the pocket of his big overcoat, took out a folded piece of paper and passed it to Ginny.

'I'm trusting that this will help,' he said. 'It's a map of sorts. It won't do the whole job, but it will go some way to it. Manawl's words for unlocking the book you already have. I hope you have not forgotten them. The problem is, they will only work if you are in the right place at the right time, and you may have to try more than once. We know no more, really, than you do yourselves. There's an element of intuition and guesswork, which only you can decipher.'

'For me?' Ginny asked as he passed it to her.

'Leo will carry the brooch,' Gido said. 'You carry the map.'

'It's stuck closed,' Ginny said, attempting to unfold the paper and look at its contents.

'You'll find it will open, when you need it,' Gido said. 'And remember this. There is more than one route to returning Manawl's treasure to the world. His knowledge and wisdom is the same, and more, than I took from the world. All I can tell you is: go to a stone circle, choose a good moon, and start there…'

'Hang on,' Leo said. 'You haven't told us…'

'I've told you all there is to tell,' Gido said. 'Remember that, until you ensure the safety of the book in the real world, Maria and I will remain in Dreamworld – half way to our destiny – so, please… you have done so well, so well, so far…'

'Don't let us down,' Maria said, and her voice seemed to grow faint and her strange Dreamworld accent was reappearing.

Maria put out her hand to Ginny.

'Good luck, my liddle maid,' she said.

'Good-bye,' Gido said. 'We will find a way to repay you for all you have done.'

They smiled as though it really was a regretful parting, perhaps the last ever.

Ginny smiled in return. No matter how awful some of the experiences they'd shared, she would never forget them.

'Come on!' Maria put her hand on Gido's arm and her voice was urgent.

She looked up at the sky and pointed.

They followed her gaze. They stared hard at the stars and the moon, and their eyes roved across the entire sky, but they saw nothing that seemed to relate to Maria's panic.

'What? Where?' Leo asked eventually. 'Is it that big, dark patch over there?' But as he looked round, he realised that only he, Ginny, Basil, and the Grolchen Rolf, were together watching the sky, and they had no idea either.

Maria and Gido were gone.

* * *

Inside the theatre, Carl was making his way from the backstage area up to the technician's gallery. He whistled quietly as he went, thinking to himself that he was a very lucky man. Before he met Rhian, he had never had anything to do with the theatre, but during the past few years, it had become a regular interest, which he thoroughly enjoyed. This was his third pantomime, and it was definitely his most successful to date.

Down in the green room, he and Rhian had managed to keep things moving smoothly throughout the evening. Make-up, wigs, hairdressing, costumes, hand props, script run-throughs, all of these had been their domain, and everyone agreed they had done a great job.

Now the final act was in progress, and he couldn't resist seeing it from a high vantage point. It was the scene where Cinderella tries on the glass slipper, and as she slipped it onto her foot, the audience cheered. The Ugly Sisters wept onto each other's shoulders, and Buttons ran about, clapping furiously, encouraging the audience to enjoy their downfall. Carl grinned to himself. The costumes were marvellous, the actors were great, the set was terrific, and the atmosphere was brilliant. He wondered if the children were enjoying it. He idly scanned the audience, looking for them.

To his surprise, where they should have been sitting were two empty seats. He could see no reason for them having moved places, as their seats were ideally placed for a perfect view of the stage, but he continued to look round, just in case.

There was no sign of them anywhere. He looked round for Ginny's mother, wondering whether they might have moved to sit nearer to her. She was sitting at the end of a row down near the front, but the children were not there. He decided to return to the Green Room, through the foyer, just to check whether or not they were there.

The foyer was more or less empty. The two women responsible for taking tickets were chatting quietly by the door, and the barman was wiping the bar, a look of boredom on his face.

He nodded to Carl as he passed.

'Show going well?' he asked, obviously glad of someone to speak to.

'Very much so,' Carl said. 'You've not seen a couple of kids hanging around, have you?'

The barman shook his head.

'All quiet and peaceful here, mate,' he said. 'There were two kids. In the first half. The girl was choking, and I gave her a glass of water. They went outside to get some fresh air, but that was hours ago. Wouldn't be them, would it?'

'I don't know,' Carl said. 'What were they like?'

'Young teenagers, I should say,' the man thought back. 'A tall lad with fair hair, and the girl, brown shoulder-length, blue jacket...' he stopped and thought. 'I did see them again, come to think of it. Just before the second half started, they went outside again. I remember thinking that if they didn't put a step on it, they wouldn't get back in time.'

'And did they?' Carl asked.

The barman shook his head.

'Didn't see,' he said. 'I was taking the empties through, so I don't know whether they came back in or not.'

Carl returned to the Green Room, where chaos was in progress. All the cast were diving into their costumes for the final scene. Rhian was helping Cinderella into the beautiful wedding dress she had spent so long making, and all around were shouts of, 'Where's my hat, Rhian?' and 'Carl, can you touch up my make-up?' and so on.

Carl did his best to help, and said nothing to Rhian about the children until the cast had disappeared in a flurry of excitement.

'I just went up to the gallery,' he said, when the door had closed behind them. 'I could see everyone in the entire auditorium. But I couldn't see our two. They weren't in their seats.'

'I'm not surprised,' Rhian said. 'Ginny didn't look too well, did she? She still had a horrible cold. P'raps she couldn't stop coughing.'

'The barman said he gave her a drink of water…' he began.

'There you are, then,' Rhian said cheerfully. 'Come on. We should get back stage, ready for our bow. You know what it's like, first night. Everybody on the stage!'

She saw that Carl looked worried, and put a hand on his shoulder.

'I'm sure there's a perfectly rational explanation,' Rhian said. 'Don't you think you might be over-reacting? I know how worried you were when she went missing, but I'm sure they're okay.'

'I expect so,' Carl replied. 'But when the two of them get together… I don't know which of them leads the other one on. I remember when they went off at the standing stones. We never got to the bottom of that little escapade, did we?'

Rhian looked confused.

'I don't remember,' she said. 'Whatever made you bring that up now? It's all of two years ago.'

'It may well be,' Carl said. 'It's just that I had this feeling then, that there's something going on we don't know about.'

'You're worrying about nothing.' Rhian said, smiling at him. 'Don't let it spoil things. Maybe, Sara saw them leave, or maybe, they told her where they were going. Leo's too sensible for them to have gone far. They probably moved seats, when they came back in. We'll find out at the end of the show.'

It was some time later, after finishing their duties, that Rhian and Carl made their way round to the foyer to meet Sara and, they hoped, the two children.

Sara was standing alone near the outside doors, watching people leaving.

When she saw Carl and Rhian, she called across to them, 'Are they with you?'

Carl shook his head.

'We don't know where they are,' Rhian said, when they reached her. 'Didn't they go in when you did?'

'The last thing I know was Ginny asked me was for the car keys because she was hot,' Sara said. 'I thought it was a bit odd, that she wanted to put her scarf in the car, but I didn't want to start an argument in the queue. I haven't seen them since. I assumed they'd come in and taken up their seats somewhere behind me.'

They all looked at each other.

'I was at the front, you see...' Sara faltered. 'So I wouldn't have seen them if they didn't... I mean...'

'I know what you mean,' Rhian said.

She moved to look beyond where Sara stood, out into the dark night. The headlights of cars leaving the car park swept past, lighting up the road as they went.

'Why would they want the car keys?' she asked. 'Maybe you should go and check that your car is still there.'

'Well, neither of them can drive, can they?' Carl said, as though it was a silly idea.

'I can't think why they would want it, unless they wanted to let the dogs out for a walk, or something,' Sara answered. 'Ginny had been feeling a bit claustrophobic; that's why she wasn't in for the first half.'

'What?' Carl and Rhian glanced at each other, surprised.

'We thought it was her cough,' Carl said.

'Whatever it was, she was outside when I arrived, about ten minutes after the show started. Then we bumped into Leo and we put the two dogs in the back of the car...'

'Two dogs?' Carl asked. 'You've got two again, have you?'

'No,' Sara said. 'I wish I had. I've still just got little Basil. I'd love that one you're looking after for your foreign friends. He's a beauty, he is. Just like Rolf. Anyway, Leo was walking him, when we put Basil in the car, and he jumped in with him, just like that. So I said, leave them there together. No problem.'

'We are looking after a dog for foreign friends?' Rhian queried, with a funny look.

'Yes, well, that's what Leo said. They live a long way off, that's how he's got such a funny name. Grolchen, wasn't it? He's lovely he is. I...'

'We don't have foreign friends with a dog,' Carl said. 'And we're not looking after any dog for anyone, and the name Grolchen means nothing to us.'

Precisely at that moment, Rolf the Grolchen entered the foyer, bounced straight up to Ginny's mum, as though to his owner, and sat at her feet, looking up at her with an adoring obedient expression.

'This is him,' Sara said, smiling and stretching out a hand to stroke the beautiful head.

Following him only moments later, from out of the darkness, came Basil, then Leo, then Ginny.

'Oh, no,' groaned Leo, seeing the ring of questioning faces that awaited them.

'Hi,' Ginny said, attempting a casual note.

'So, what's going on?' Carl asked, and they couldn't help thinking he didn't look very happy at all. 'Did you see any of the show?'

Ginny and Leo looked at each other.

Ginny shook her head.

'Ginny wasn't well...' Leo began.

'Look,' Rhian intervened hastily, aware that most of the stage company were congregating around them, ready for their late evening meal. 'We're all going to the restaurant now, and we are not going to let you two out of our sight! Got it?'

They nodded, accepting that now they could relax and let matters take their course, even if it meant a lecture later.

'We'll talk about this,' Carl said sternly, 'when we get home.'

Chapter 9

Stones and Surprises

It was Sunday, the day after the evening of the pantomime, and Leo and Ginny were in the cosy front room of Ginny's house.

Outside, the day was fading to dusk and a cold wind blew. Along the roadway an edging of white betrayed where the snow of the night before had stuck and frozen, and added to a scene that was wintry and chill.

Inside, it was warm and bright. The Christmas tree, which stood in the corner, glittering with shiny baubles and winking lights, filled the air with the smell of pine, and lit up the colourful decorations and greenery around the room. Christmas cards covered every surface, and here and there a wrapped parcel, dropped in by a friend or a relative, held the promise of something exciting to come.

Leo lay on the sofa with an open book, but his eyes were glazed and not focussed on the page. Ginny was sitting at the dining table. She had just read a message inside a Christmas card from Gwen, the Games Captain, confirming her place on the Athletics Team the following term. Jules had told Ginny that, on the last day of term, the whole school was talking about nothing else but her lying outside the castle with a bat on her face. She was a celebrity, and Gwen, in her kind note, said she had heard how brave Ginny had been, and was impressed. It was a piece of good news, which might normally have had her turning cartwheels, but instead, she started doing a puzzle in a magazine.

She and Leo were grounded, and making the best of it.

'We're not going to be able to get there,' Leo said. 'There's no way they'll take us up to Gors Fawr, after everything else.'

'No,' Ginny said. 'They think we can't be trusted.'

'We can't, can we?' Leo said, 'because, the minute their backs are turned, we're doing things we can't tell them about. Mind you, now the last of the gruesome trio is gone…'

'What a relief!' Ginny said.

'Just think, all we have to do now is follow a map and get rid of Manawl's brooch,' Leo said. 'I used to think I wanted to keep it, but now I'll be glad to see the back of it and get life back to normal.'

'Me, too,' Ginny murmured. 'But saying 'all we have to do' makes it sound easy, and I somehow don't think it will be.'

'It can't be that difficult,' Leo mused. 'But it would be good to get it out of the way, and I don't see how we can, while we're being treated like criminals. Honestly, I never thought they would be so angry about us missing the pantomime. I thought everyone would just be kind and understanding, when you said you'd been claustrophobic. Instead, we're stuck doing boring things.'

'But they were angry because they were worried. You know that,' Ginny sighed, looking up from her puzzle. 'They didn't know where we'd been, and we didn't explain it very well, did we? When you said we went outside for a breath of air for me, and suddenly an old friend of yours, who nobody had ever heard of, gave you his dog on his way to catching a plane to Australia, and said, "Please find him a good home because I'm not coming back." I couldn't bear to watch their faces. I wanted to laugh, but I knew we were in big trouble, because they didn't believe a word of it!'

'I thought they swallowed that quite reasonably,' Leo said, but he remembered their boggling faces and knew they hadn't. 'I couldn't come up with anything better, at short notice. And now, the worst thing is, I daren't ask them to take us up to Gors Fawr, to get rid of the brooch. Can you imagine Carl's face? All that stuff about 'suspicious behaviour', and he even brought it up – about when we went missing before!'

'And my mum joined in, saying that she thought we'd been up to no good, when we went to Newport!' Ginny added. 'But she won't stay cross, because she's got the Grolchen. It's just Carl and Rhian. I think we've hurt their feelings. They worked so hard on the pantomime and, even though we said we'd really like them to take us again, they didn't believe us.'

'I know,' Leo agreed. 'But we didn't hurt them on purpose. They'll get over it, and we did get rid of the last Dreamstealer, instead of sitting watching their production. Which is more important to the world, I ask you?'

Ginny laughed.

The thought that all three of the dreaded Undead from the Cauldron were gone forever still filled her with unspeakable joy and relief.

'But while we sit on the brooch,' Leo continued, 'Gido and Maria are hanging about, waiting for us to do something. All the Stealers are gone from the world, and they could move on now, but we've got the brooch and they won't go until we get it to the right place. I wonder what moving to the next dimension is like.

I mean, I wonder if they're standing on a platform somewhere, waiting for the train to Annwn.'

'Leo, don't make jokes about it. It makes me feel weird. I hate the thought that we're holding them up,' Ginny said, becoming serious. 'Maybe we should grovel to dad and Rhian, try and think up a better story to explain the Grolchen.'

'There is no better story,' Leo said. 'Whatever we tell them now, they won't believe. He was too much for them.'

It was true that the Grolchen had upset Carl and Rhian.

Here was an animal whose sudden appearance could not be explained and who seemed to understand every word that human beings said, who sat with his head on one side, resting on a paw, listening in and looking from one to another.

As if this wasn't enough, Rhian was almost certain that, when the dog caught her eye, she saw it smile and wink, though how a dog could be said to do either of those things she wasn't sure.

The fact that Sara had more than happily said she would take responsibility for the creature went some way to calm things down, and had been received with evident relief.

Leo's excuse for appearing with a dog at all was so ludicrous that, though it was accepted, it was only because there was no evidence for any alternative theory.

And in the end, it had been agreed that, for the next few days, Leo would be grounded at Ginny's house, under Sara's eye, whilst Carl and Rhian fulfilled their obligations at the theatre.

'We can't trust you on your own,' Rhian had said. 'We have to be out every evening for the coming week, and we're out at work during the day. You think you can appear and disappear as you please, and then you turn up with a strange dog. You ignore all our hard work and walk out on the production, which is insulting to Carl and myself, and, to top it all, instead of bringing Ginny to the Green Room, if she really wasn't well, you take her outside, late at night, in the freezing cold, to goodness knows where, after what she'd been through.'

Leo had tried hard to look suitably penitent, in the hope that he would be allowed to simply be grounded at home, but his mother wasn't co-operating.

'So now you can stay at Ginny's, where Sara can keep an eye on you both,' she'd continued. 'She'll bring you both back on Christmas Eve, and we'll all have Christmas Day together. Carl has told Sara she can bring the dogs with her, though how we'll manage with such a houseful, I don't know. Anyway, they all go back on Boxing Day because they're going to stay with Ginny's Aunt Izzy.'

Leo thought about it and concluded that, obviously, if Ginny was going away after Christmas, it would be best if they could do the job with the brooch soon, and get it out of the way.

Gido's map, on its folded piece of paper, had still not been opened. It seemed to be glued together in much the same way as an envelope, and they had not yet had much opportunity to examine it.

Leo was just about to ask Ginny if he could have another look at it, when the door opened and Ginny's mum looked in on them.

'I've just had a call from your mother,' she said to Leo. 'She said to tell you that your friend has been taken into care.'

'What?' Leo asked, startled.

'Your friend Boris,' Sara came into the room and sat on the arm of a chair.

She obviously believed that Bos was a close friend of Leo's, and her voice was sympathetic and kind.

'It's very sad, isn't it? Last night, the police found him sleeping outside, and they discovered that he's been living rough for months,' she said. 'They contacted your mother, because he said you were his best friend and could vouch for who he was.'

'Best friend!' Leo was about to protest, but it stuck in his throat.

He suddenly knew that, since Bos's father had died in the summer, Bos had been living from hand to mouth, with no-one to look after him and no home to go to. The Stealer had presumably been the mythical 'uncle', who gave him money from time to time, and now he was gone, there was no-one. He didn't know what to say.

Ginny's mum mistook his discomfort for sadness, and continued with her story, which had, it seemed, a happy ending.

'Don't worry about him any more, Leo,' she said. 'They've found him a nice place, with a kind foster family, where he'll be looked after properly. Just in time for Christmas, too… Apparently, he was getting into bad ways…'

'I know,' Leo said, and from somewhere came the memory of the day when Leo had gone to Bos's horrible home, to get some money back from him, and the claw like hand of the dreadful parent had reached out to snatch it.

He was glad Bos didn't have to live with that, at least. He didn't like him any more today than he ever had, but he was glad that, maybe, his life would be better.

'Thanks for telling me, anyway,' he said, wanting to end the conversation.

'I've put some food out in the kitchen, for when you want it,' Sara said. 'I'm going to watch the film that's just starting. You can come and watch it with me if you like, but I expect you want to get on with your own things, don't you?'

'Thanks,' Leo said. 'I don't want to watch a film, but I am quite hungry.'

He got up and stretched his legs.

'But first, maybe we could walk the dogs for you, before it gets dark?'

Sara looked uncertain.

She wanted to stick to her promise to Rhian, which had been to make sure that Leo knew he was being punished for worrying everyone. But Sara couldn't feel anything but gratitude and affection for Leo, because it was he who had brought her the Grolchen.

Grolchen, as she would always know him now, was the most intelligent dog she had ever dreamed of owning, and he reminded her of Rolf. She wondered who had trained him. Only that morning, he had climbed up on to the piano stool, turned to make sure she was watching, and proceeded to pick out what sounded remarkably like a tune, whilst seeming to hum along to it. She just knew that there were going to be lots more discoveries ahead about his skills, that he would be the friend Basil needed, and would bring happiness into their lives. And she had Leo to thank.

'I think they could do with a little walk,' she agreed after a pause. 'But you won't go far, will you, and you won't linger out too long if it gets dark.'

'Right,' Leo said, grinning and turning to Ginny. 'Coming?'

★ ★ ★

Once across the little bridge that spanned the River Mwldan, they let the dogs off their leads and they raced ahead.

'I've not been this way before,' Leo said.

'It just goes up the Estuary – Basil likes it up here, so I expect the Grolchen will too,' Ginny said.

As they came down the path, which widened and opened on to a green space, the dogs changed direction and turned back, slowing down to join the children. Both Basil and Grolchen then held to their heels, as though they were waiting to see where they would go, not wanting to be left behind.

'What's up with them?' Leo asked. 'They don't usually walk to heel for no reason, do they?'

'Basil always does it, when we get to this point. I guess it must be that,' Ginny said, pointing. 'Look. There, just up ahead.'

On the patch of green that was part of a recreation ground, between bandstands and children's play equipment, stood a stone circle, which spanned an area of perhaps twenty or so metres. Some of the stones were as tall as a man, whilst others were less impressive in height but were, nonetheless, bulky and significant monoliths. As a whole, the circle had a presence, which obviously intimidated the dogs.

Leo stopped, his mouth wide open.

'I don't believe it!' he cried. 'That's amazing.'

'Not really,' Ginny said, continuing to walk towards s it. 'It's not a real one!'

'What d'you mean?' Leo asked. 'It's a circle made of stones. That makes it a stone circle, doesn't it?'

'Yes, but it's modern,' Ginny said. 'It's not ancient like Gors Fawr...'

'Ginny! It's a stone circle!' Leo shouted, and he was becoming excited. 'It doesn't matter whether it's old or new. It only matters that it is what it is. Gido didn't say go to Gors Fawr, and even if he had, we've got no chance of getting there this side of Christmas! He said go to a stone circle! This is a stone circle. How many stone circles are there, for goodness sake? Not that many, and this looks very convincing to me. They're big stones, too, bigger than Gors Fawr. I think it looks great. Get the map out, and let's see if we can get it open. If we can... !'

He walked into the circle, and the dogs, seeing him walk there unafraid, seemed to lose their uncertainty, and ran about again, as though Leo had broken some kind of spell.

He wandered between the stones, touching those he passed close to, enjoying the sensation of being in what he felt to be an extraordinary space. It didn't matter to him that Ginny thought it was not real because of its age. In the centre was a large squat stone slab, on which he sat now and waited for Ginny, who was fumbling in her pockets, trying to find the piece of folded paper.

He looked up at the sky and then down towards the water of the estuary. Everything seemed bathed in a pale silvery light as the day moved towards dusk.

'This is fantastic,' Leo said, and he was filled with elation, brief but wonderful. Even the cold couldn't penetrate his inner warmth, to cut short his enjoyment.

'This is the place to start,' he said with certainty. 'It's meant to be. You remember when we went to Cilgerran Castle and Gido told us that there is a power of place that attracts us. I think he was right and this is what he meant. We needed a stone circle and here we are, walking right into one. Can you beat that? We could have walked a different way, but we didn't. How come there's a stone circle in the middle of the town anyway? I don't understand it. It's like it was put here especially for us.'

'Well it wasn't,' Ginny said finally finding the map in the last pocket she'd searched. 'It was made for an Eisteddfod, years ago, not hundreds of years, you know, only when my mum was young, But it was in the way of some building work, or something, where it was, so they moved it here because people in the town didn't want it to be pulled down. I don't know why, but it's been here ever since.'

She pulled at the folded paper, which she had tried to open earlier with no success, and it opened readily.

'Look at that,' she said, surprised and delighted.

'What does it say?'

Ginny read it aloud, 'Walk three rings widdershins with words from Annwn, lay metal on stone and wait the bell.'

'What else.'

Ginny turned the paper over.

'Nothing.'

'Are you telling me that's it?' Leo's voice rose in annoyance, his happy mood of conviction that everything was going to fall readily into place vanishing in seconds. 'The whole so-called map? That isn't a map, that's just stupid.'

'I can't help it!' Ginny cried. 'Don't shout at me. It's not my fault that's all there is.'

Leo sat, holding his head in his hands.

'I don't believe this,' he said. 'We find a stone circle, like we're told, and the map is a load of rubbish. Read it again, slowly this time.'

'Walk three rings widdershins…'

'Wait,' Leo cried. 'What was that word?'

'Widdershins,' Ginny answered. 'It means anti-clockwise. I know that. I've read it somewhere and 'with words from Annwn' means saying what Manawl told us.'

'Okay, okay,' Leo said, and he sighed with frustration. 'I suppose we can give it a try. Why does Gido always tell us as little as possible? Honestly, it makes me mad.'

He began to pace anti-clockwise around inside the stones, starting at the tallest one, so he would know it again when he had completed a circle, then counted three circuits whilst mumbling the words Manawl had spoken under his breath. They had not been long or difficult words, but Leo had wondered from time to time, since the day they'd received them, whether he had remembered them correctly. He supposed now would be the time he would find out. If he got it wrong, Ginny would have to take a turn.

When he'd finished, he turned to Ginny, who was pacing around outside the circle, keeping herself warm and watching out for the dogs.

'Right, what was next?' he asked.

'Lay metal on stone and wait the bell.' she said. 'And hurry up. I'm freezing.'

'What bell?'

'No idea,' Ginny replied. 'But I think Gido might have told us if he meant us to bring one.'

'All right,' Leo drew the brooch from his pocket. It was warm but still looked like a flat tin lid. 'Do you think when it says 'lay metal' it means the brooch?'

Ginny shrugged. She didn't know and was beginning to wonder whether they shouldn't get back. The dogs had begun to hover around her legs, as though even they were feeling chilly and were ready to go home.

She didn't have Leo's confidence that the stone circle would do any magic, and felt impatient with him. It wasn't ancient and, in the past, she had actually sat in it with friends, eating fish and chips and watching the boats on the river. Children played in it, and teenagers congregated in it in the evenings in summer, and to her, it wasn't a real stone circle at all.

Not like Gors Fawr, which she felt certain was what Gido had meant. Gors Fawr was the place where, all those centuries ago, he had buried the old knowledge. It was a special spot that had old magic in it, and going there would make some kind of sense. But this just felt as though they were playing a kid's game, and it was getting dark, and her mum would be worrying if they were out much longer.

She bit her lip and said nothing. Let Leo find out for himself that there was no magic, and then they would get back and have some food. She, too, looked at the sky and was surprised to see that the moon had appeared and there was a ring around it that looked like a halo. She wondered whether that meant temperatures were dropping to freezing. It certainly felt like it.

She pointed to it.

'He did say choose a good moon. D'you think that's a good one?'

Leo looked up and whistled.

'Wowee, that's a corker,' he said. 'I haven't got any other metal on me, so it'll have to be this. That must be what he meant.'

He laid the brooch on the slab of stone in the centre of the circle.

'Now… ?' Leo looked up as if about to ask a question, but before he could say it, there was a noise like the bang of an enormous gong.

The sound reverberated across and up and down the river and echoed into the distance. The dogs both barked aloud in shock, and then stood quivering, noses up, ears pricked, waiting for what might follow.

As if in a dream, Leo saw Gido and Maria in the stone circle, holding hands, smiling at him. It was early summer and there were dandelions and daisies sprinkling the grass, and birds were whizzing about in the leafy trees, and both the Keepers looked quite different, not funny or odd, but a handsome couple, and there were people, people as far as the eye could see, in gorgeous clothes and glittering colours, like at a wedding…

He gasped in amazement, raised an arm to point at it, and it was gone.

The sound, though, was real and was still vibrating through the air, even if the images had vanished.

'The sound of the bell,' he cried to Ginny. 'What did you see?'

Ginny was stupefied, wondering where on earth the noise had come from and what was going to happen next. Standing on the outside of the circle, she had seen nothing other than Leo's saucer-like eyes and the raised pointing arm.

'I saw you looking like a startled rabbit,' she said, 'and I heard that noise! If it was a bell, it was a big one.'

'Was that from a church, or something?' Leo asked.

'How should I know?' Ginny asked.

'You live here,' Leo answered. 'Haven't you heard it before? I thought I saw Gido and Maria – happy, together... with all their friends. Didn't you see them?'

Ginny shook her head.

'I told you. I didn't see anything. But that noise was definitely not the church. It's right over the other side of town.'

She glanced downriver, across the water, and for some reason, she thought of the ruins of the ancient abbey at St Dogmael's. If Leo believed he'd seen Gido and Maria, she could tease him just a little.

'It's the ghostly bell of the 13th century abbey ruins,' she said. 'Everybody round here knows about that.'

Leo looked at her sharply.

'Is that genuine, or are you messing about?' he asked.

Ginny crossed her fingers behind her back. She was a bit disappointed that Leo had seen something she had not.

'It sounded to me like the abbey bell,' she said, enjoying her moment of teasing.

'Of course it was,' said a voice from behind her. 'Though, how you guessed I can't imagine.'

Ginny yelped aloud and jumped, turning to see who it was, whilst Leo took a sudden step backwards in surprise. He had seen someone approaching behind Ginny, but it wasn't until he got close that he saw who it was.

The voice came from Mr Evans, his teacher, who had suddenly appeared from the top path that led down from the road, where there was a skateboard park. He was holding a small remote control panel of the sort they knew operated model cars and planes.

The dogs showed no defensive behaviour, but headed towards him in a friendly, sniffy, doggy way.

'Good though, wasn't it?' Mr Evans asked, beaming. 'I'm sorry if I startled you. It's good to see you both again. I wondered what happened to you the other night, but I see you are both well. I was just trying out my latest home-made toy. I should have turned the volume down but I didn't know anyone was about. At such high decibels, the distortion is fantastic but interesting.'

He saw their confusion.

'I collect sounds,' he said, pointing to his gadget. 'And then I replicate them at different volumes and speeds, in an attempt to disarrange our perspective of reality. When it comes to ancient sounds, like the abbey bell, you can only collect them from the river bed and...'

Ginny raised her eyebrows and looked sideways at Leo, wondering what he made of this. Leo didn't know what to think. Mr Evans seemed to sense their uncertainty and stepped back.

'I'm talking a lot of what to you must sound like rubbish,' he said. 'I get carried away and forget that others are not as preoccupied with discovery as I am. I promised to tell you what I was researching, Leo. So now you know.'

Then, over his shoulder,

'Jack!' he yelled.

The boy they had met at the theatre rounded the corner on a skateboard, jumped off it and, with a confident flick of the wrist, tipped it into the air and caught it, before walking towards s them.

'You missed the panto,' he called. 'It was really good.'

Leo's first thought was that he wouldn't mind learning how to do what he had just seen Jack do. A week in Cardigan might not be so bad after all.

'I'm staying with Jack and his mum for the holidays,' Mr Evans said. 'So I thought I'd make use of being on different territory to experiment with this.'

Jack grinned at them cheerfully and stroked the dogs, which had approached him in their usual friendly manner.

'So, tell me how you guessed what the sound was,' Mr Evans asked Ginny.

Ginny smiled a slightly embarrassed smile, not sure what to say.

'It was kind of a joke,' she said.

'An intuitive guess, I imagine,' Mr Evans said, 'which always impresses me! So many of the spontaneous things we say come from the old knowledge that is stored in our subconscious minds, and a stone circle is as good a place as any for it to happen!'

'This is not an ancient place, though,' Ginny said hurriedly.

'The place, of course, is ancient,' Mr Evans laughed. 'What you mean is, the stone circle on the place is not. Thank you for telling me, but like you, I know it is a 20th century circle. However, I believe all stone circles are magic in their own way... and the places we choose to put them often have a special atmosphere.'

'That's just what I said,' Leo said. 'Something about them standing here together in a circle makes me think they're kind of talking to each other.'

'How right you are,' Mr Evans said, 'and not simply to each other, but to us... to the human world... batteries... generators...

and that power is added to by us positioning them in certain places...'

'How could you do what you said?' Leo asked, interrupting what promised to be a long explanation. 'How could you find the sound of a bell from centuries ago in the river bed?'

'It's what I do,' Mr Evans replied. 'I'm a bit of an inventor. I use imprints of sound from the past – river beds are a good place, so are stones, of course. Everything that happens on the planet leaves a reverberation, a sound which is left trapped until we decode it. We don't think it odd that we can find fossils locked in stone, which tell us of life forms in the distant past, do we? Well, I look for, and collect, fossil sounds from the past. They're harder to find but well worth the effort!'

The two children must have looked slightly bewildered because he carried on with his explanation.

'What I'm actually doing is searching for the very particular sound which, when replicated, will draw back the veil and allow us a glimpse of dimensions other than the solid one which we inhabit. That, Leo, is why I'm so lucky to have a copy of The Escalado and why I never let it out of my sight. He seems to think that, a long time ago, we knew the way to do that. I'm sure he's right. We knew how to shout or whisper across the boundary, and we've lost the information, the science, as it were...'

Leo found himself wondering whether the bell sound had brought the image of Maria and Gido into the circle, and thought that maybe Mr Evans was closer to finding the sound he was looking for than he knew. Leo couldn't help thinking what Rhian and Carl's response to him would be.

'Don't most people think you're mad,' he asked.

Mr Evans laughed at his question.

'I don't talk about it a great deal, for that very reason!' he said. 'But then, someone has to be the first to find things out, don't they. If I'm wrong, so what? It's only my time I'm wasting!'

'Why don't you try it in the circle?' Leo asked.

He didn't say what he had seen, but he hoped that something similar might happen.

'Why not,' Mr Evans said, striding towards him.

Leo beckoned Ginny 'Come on,' he said. 'Let's all stand in the circle. Just to see what happens.'

'I think we should be going,' she said. 'My mum gets worried if we're out too long.'

'Two minutes,' Leo said.

Reluctantly, Ginny walked into the circle. She was frozen stiff and somehow a little afraid of what might happen.

Jack followed, carrying his skateboard, and they stood together, whilst Mr Evans twiddled the controls on his gadget.

The second clang of the bell was not as loud, but it went on for longer.

For several seconds, they all stood listening, and Ginny and Leo saw, laid over the cold winter ground, as though looking at a reflection in water, Spring with all its life and colour, and people, lots of people.

'Gido, Maria!' Ginny shouted to Leo. 'I saw them!'

The images disappeared. Mr Evans looked stunned. Jack was capering about, laughing.

'See!' he chortled. 'When it works, you don't know what to do!'

'Did you see something?' Mr Evans asked the children. 'I

could have sworn I saw something… a different time… a different place.'

'I did,' Jack said. 'It was like summer… like a reflection in water. I could've imagined it though.'

'Maybe you've found a sound you've been looking for,' Leo said to Mr Evans, who looked dazed and bewildered.

Leo turned to Ginny. She was blue with cold, and though she was smiling in a weepy kind of way, he felt guilty about keeping her hanging about.

'We'll have to go,' he said to Mr Evans, who had not moved from where he stood in the circle, still taking in what had happened.

'See you again,' they called as they rounded up the dogs and set off down the path towards home.

Mr Evans called after them.

'Hang on. You've left something here on the stone.'

Leo's stunned face turned to see Ginny's startled gaze fixed on him.

'You forgot the brooch!' she cried. 'How could you? How could you? All that messing about and reading the map and then you forgot it.'

'So did you,' Leo said. 'You didn't think about it either, so it's just a good job he found it! I'll run and get it!'

He turned to run, and Ginny turned with him. In the fading light, there was a brief brightness, as though the moon with its white halo of frosty promise threw down a handful of sparks to light up what was in front of them. Like a spotlight, it shone down on Mr Evans, standing in the centre of the circle. They could see him waving a large book, silhouetted against the sky.

Neither spoke, though both drew a quick breath of surprise. It needed no discussion. They knew what they were seeing. They walked back towards him, side by side, with the dogs at their heels, in unbelieving silence.

'Do you mind my asking where you got this?' Mr Evans asked, when they came near enough to hear him speak without shouting. 'I know you're interested in old books, Leo, but this is extraordinary.'

In the dusk, he squinted at the title on the front.

'Defnydd Hud. It's a magical textbook, and a very old one, if I'm not mistaken. It shouldn't be left lying around outside on a frosty night!'

All both children could think about was whether the book would stay a book or whether it would suddenly turn back into a tin lid, but in Mr Evans' hands, it seemed to have a solidity which was convincing and real.

They were tongue-tied and when Mr Evans tried to pass the book to Leo, Leo did not reach out for it. Neither did Ginny.

'It is yours, isn't it?' Mr Evans asked.

'No,' Leo said, shaking his head. And he knew without a doubt that it was the right answer.

He knew it was meant for Mr Evans and not for him. Otherwise, he would not have appeared and rung the magical bell. The map had worked in every way. How amazing.

'No. It isn't ours,' Ginny said, and Leo, looking at her knew she understood too.

'But you're right about it not being left outside,' she continued. 'Maybe you should take it home and look after it.'

'I would very much like to do that,' Mr Evans said, and he stroked the book, looking at it in something approaching disbelief. 'But the owner will be worried about where it's got to.'

'If someone has lost it,' Leo said. 'They'll ask the police, won't they?'

'Yes, yes,' Mr Evans replied. 'Of course. I shall report finding it. Quite right. I'm sorry I delayed you.'

He turned and with the book he made a kind of salute in the air. As he walked off, Jack caught up with him and they disappeared on their way.

'Shall we go home now?' Leo asked Ginny.

She beamed at him and, in the dark, he could see her white teeth.

'What a super way for it to happen,' she said. 'I can hardly believe it. After all those things you said about it being a useless map!'

Leo chuckled.

'But, Mr Evans! I'd no idea he was so... you know... unusual.'

Ginny laughed.

Leo looked at her in surprise.

'What's funny?' he asked.

'Everything,' she giggled. 'The Grolchen coming back for my mum, the book being in the right hands, the Stealers all gone, the Keepers happy, my place on the team, your friend Bos being looked after, Christmas, pantomimes, dreams coming true...'

And then Leo found he was laughing too, because life was good, and everything had come together in the end.

'And if you think he's unusual,' Ginny said, 'what about you! Maybe he'll teach you to use it one day.'

And Leo thought that would be a perfectly brilliant idea.

* * *

Christmas morning, and the little house in Narberth was full to bursting. Rhian, Carl and Sara were in the kitchen, preparing Christmas Dinner, with lots of laughter and good humour. The two dogs were on the rug in the sitting room, and Leo and Ginny were laying the big table in the dining room with the best cutlery and glasses, discussing the gifts they had received. Both had been thrilled with their presents but, more than anything, they were happy that the bad atmosphere created by their truancy from the pantomime had lifted.

A ring on the door-bell made Leo look up in surprise.

'I'll go,' he shouted towards the kitchen.

And to Ginny he said, 'It'll be a neighbour, run out of milk or something.'

But it wasn't. On the doorstep was a youngish man with large expressive eyes, wearing a smart blue uniform. In his arms were two parcels.

'Courier,' he said smartly. He was grinning his head off. He pushed a clipboard with a piece of paper on it towards Leo. 'Sign here please.'

The way he was smiling suggested it might be a joke, and Leo hesitated.

'Who are they for?' he asked. 'I should ask my mum to…'

'No, no,' the youth interrupted. 'They are for you, and your sister.'

He waved the clipboard again at Leo and Leo took it from him.

'On Christmas Day?' Leo asked uncertainly.

He looked down at the paper, which had a pen attached to it, and on it were the words. 'Museum of Rare Coins.'

'There's been a mistake,' Leo mumbled. 'I don't have any rare coins.'

'But you did have,' smiled the young man, 'didn't you?'

Something about the way he said it made Leo look twice at him.

'Who are you?' he asked. 'Where are you from?'

The courier put his finger to his lips.

'Ssh. Please, sign it,' then he whispered. 'I really want your autographs. I can't tell you where I'm from, only that Gido sent me.'

Behind Leo, the rest of the family, alerted by the fact that Leo was still on the doorstep, gathered in the hallway, first Ginny, then Rhian, then Carl and Sara, all drawn to the door, to see what was going on.

'Courier from the Museum of Coins,' the young man saluted them, smiling happily. 'Your two children have been awarded a special gift for an old coin they found.'

'Good heavens!' Rhian said.

Ginny stood open-mouthed as Leo signed the paper.

The young man then thrust it into her hands.

'Yours, too, please,' he said.

She hesitated.

'From Gido,' he whispered, so no-one else would hear.

Ginny signed it.

She stared at the courier. She knew he was staring at her too, as someone might stare at a film star.

She blushed.

'Thank you so much,' he said, taking back the clipboard and passing the parcels to them.

'Merry Christmas to you all.'

And with a wave, he headed off up the street and disappeared.

'You never told us about a rare coin,' Carl began.

'No,' Leo answered quickly. 'We didn't know if it was rare, so I gave it to Mr Evans, my teacher, and he…'

'Well, fancy that,' Sara said.

'Ooh, how exciting,' Rhian said. 'Come on, open them up. Let's see what they've sent you.'

Back indoors, everyone gathered round, whilst the two children opened the parcels.

Both were slightly nervous of unwrapping them, thinking they might contain something so odd that the parents would start asking questions again.

Leo's parcel came open first.

'Oh, wow!' he cried. 'Look at that!'

He lifted out a skateboard, with beautiful symbols, and his name painted in luminous colours on it.

'Just exactly what I wanted,' he said. 'Now I'll be able to keep up with Jack!'

As the wrapping fell away, it hit the floor with a thud, and Rhian stooped to see what else there was.

'There's a book, too,' she said. 'Look.'

It was a brand new, shiny copy of Procton's Escalado, and when Leo opened it, the fly-leaf bore the words: 'With many thanks to Leo from the Keepers and friends.'

'I suppose that means the Museum Keepers,' Carl said, looking over his shoulder. 'That looks an interesting book, Leo.'

'Yes,' Leo said, gazing at both gifts in disbelief. 'I think it is.'

Ginny was opening her parcel. Having seen Leo's, she was sure now that it was not going to be something peculiar.

She held her breath as a shimmering athletics costume, in iridescent colours, and matching training shoes emerged. Ginny squealed with delight as she held them up.

'Look! They're the same as they wear at the Olympics, and the trainers – they're like hundreds of pounds a pair!'

Beneath them, in the parcel, was a book and, as Ginny lifted it out, she saw the title; a single word: Dreamworld.

With heart beating, she opened it. Like Leo's, it was inscribed with thanks from the Keepers, and as she flicked through it, she saw there were different stories and one of them was called Farewell to the Dreamstealers. She knew at once that this was a story about herself and Leo and, not wanting everybody to see, she closed it. She and Leo would both read it later. The thought was exciting.

'My goodness,' Rhian said, beaming at them. 'How lovely! What a surprise.'

'They must have been really grateful to you,' Sara said. 'I've never heard of a Christmas Day delivery before.'

'Well done,' Carl said. 'Well done both of you.'

Then he gave a big sigh, smiling and shaking his head.

'I guess I will never, ever know what you two will get up to next!'

And if pushed, both Leo and Ginny would have been forced to admit that they didn't even know themselves.

The Cauldron of the Undead

This is the story, adapted from the Mabinogi, which originally inspired the idea of the DreamsStealers.

Long ago, in the days when Wales was ruled by the Mighty King Bran, an ugly pair of sea-faring beggars arrived one night on the coast of Wales. Those who saw them as they came in to land ran in shock and fear, shouting for their giant King to come and drown them.

But when King Bran arrived, the beggars called to him from their boat, waving and yelling to him, begging him to have mercy on them and let them come ashore. They knew who he was, without being told. His massive height was taller than any other man living, his biceps were the size of small pigs and his legs were the size of two hefty stone pillars. It could only be the Mighty King Bran the Blessed.

The unfortunate man in the boat shouted to him, 'King Bran, great and wonderful King of all the Western Lands, we beg you to let us come ashore here. We have been sailing for many years, and yearn to live and work on solid land.'

And his wife called after him, 'Wherever we go, great King, we are jeered at, and reviled for our horrible faces. The fear we put into those who see us is not of our doing. We mean no-one harm. We want a home, that is all, and are in despair that it cannot be!'

King Bran, not wanting to seem as though he acted without

thought, stepped closer to them and looked into their boat. It was obvious that they had collected all kinds of things with which to build their own home, and this impressed him.

Being a good, just man, he could see the unfairness of the judgment the couple suffered. His own huge height and strange appearance had often frightened people, and he knew what it felt like to be regarded as a threat.

'You may stay as long as you promise to do no man harm,' he told them, 'cause no riot, or steal from any other what does not belong to you.'

They agreed with delight, falling over themselves to thank him and indicating to him to take whatever treasure he would like from within their boat.

'All has been gathered at sea,' said the man. 'All is harvested from Neptune's realm, from wrecks and deserted and sunken islands, and though some we have brought to build our home, much of it we hope to sell, to raise money to keep us.'

Bran shook his great head. 'I would not take from your small store, though it is a kindness you have shown me to offer it, and I thank you. But what could there be that I, a King, would want? No... This is your own treasure, to begin your new life; take it and find a piece of land along this coastland, and keep to a peaceful life together.'

He began to walk away when he had made his agreement on this, but around him his men muttered. They wondered at his wisdom in letting the couple stay, but Bran spoke up to them.

'No whispering will I have on this,' he said. 'I say again that, until there is ever reason to complain of these two, I will have none make life difficult for them.'

The men lowered their eyes. They knew that Bran was right, for what man should be rejected simply for his looks?

'Greet them cordially,' Bran commanded.

The men did so, and so delighted were the two in the boat that it made them feel ashamed they had been so afraid of them.

The couple began to give out small gifts to the men, and to show them the things in the boat they had for selling, and Bran was pleased to see that the matter was resolved.

As he turned to leave them to their bartering, the man called to him to wait, and with the help of his wife, he wrestled a huge cauldron from the bottom of the boat and onto the ground beside it.

'This cauldron,' said the man, his gruesome face alight with wonder, 'came up from the silt-bed of the ocean, caught in one of our nets. When we lifted it from its resting place, the sky went dark, and thunder and lightning struck our boat. A voice, though there was no-one there, boomed at us through the thunder!'

His eyes were popping from their sockets as he told the tale.

'You believe me, good King?'

Bran nodded. 'What did the voice say?' he asked.

'Beware the cauldron of the undead!' the man cried.

A silence fell, and the guards beside Bran moved silently closer, to see the strange object.

'This is surely fit gift for a King such as you!' the man continued.

Bran stared at it. 'Can it be...?'

'The cauldron of Ceridwen, of life and death and the Undead!' cackled the man, his face nearly splitting in half with glee, to see

King Bran so amazed. 'No doubt it was Neptune's voice I heard, for it was Neptune who claimed the cauldron when it was thrown into his depths, and it was Neptune who alone could claim the souls of the undead. You must have heard of it in legend.'

'I have heard of it,' Bran said with quiet dread.

'It is said,' the man continued, 'that if it is put to stand over a hot fire and the dead bodies of soldiers killed in battle are thrown into it, the dead will rise from it as a new army, without flesh, only bones, with life fed back into them by the magic of the cauldron. Then, they can never die! You will always have armies greater than your enemy. Your army can never grow smaller!'

Bran was awed at the power of this gift and horrified by the responsibility it brought. He had heard of the cauldron in old tales, but had always believed it nothing more than a myth invented by story-tellers to bring wonder and fear to their listeners.

He reasoned to himself that it would be wise to accept this gift, much wiser to do so than to risk it falling into hands which might not respect its magic power, or worse, use it for wicked purposes.

'I hope that I may never see cause to use its awesome power,' he said, 'but I thank you for your gift and I will accept it.'

Then, with his guards behind him struggling to carry the great weight of the cauldron, Bran returned to his castle and arranged to see his brother Manawydan, to show him his new treasure.

Manawydan was the wisest of men. As soon as he saw the Cauldron, he counselled Bran to lock the dreadful thing away until they found an appropriate time to throw it back into the ocean. He knew at once all its history, and how it condemned souls to eternal agony.

'It meddles with life and death, with the natural process through which all men must travel to get to the next world. It condemns them forever to fight, to cause mayhem,' he said. 'And what can be done with these souls when your battle is over? Where do you send them? They will go on wrecking their own land because that is what they are re-born to do... to wreck, to fight, to kill. No! No! This is a terrible thing, we must hide it. Let no-one know you have it. And when next we put out to sea, to some far place, we will take it with us and throw it back where it belongs.'

So Bran agreed to keep it under lock and key until that time, grateful for his brother's wisdom.

The sea-beggars settled peacefully into their home, Bran forgot them, and their gift, and the cauldron lay gathering dust for many years, in a hidden room deep in Bran's huge castle.

Then, without warning, the King of Ireland invaded Bran's kingdom, and for several years there were skirmishes and battles, which cost lives on both sides.

Not once during that time did either Bran or Manawydan think of using the cauldron. And if either remembered it they pushed the memory away – it was too terrible, too evil a thing to give thought to.

Peace talks were eventually entered into at Bran's castle in Gwynedd, and the Irish King, Matholwch, came to the table with his head full of trickery and revenge.

* * *

Now Bran and Manawydan had a young and lovely sister. Her name was Branwen, and the day the Irish King first caught sight of her he wanted to own her.

He was a man used to getting his own way in all things and, though he had loved many ladies in his kingdom, he had never married. He watched Branwen as they sat at supper on his first evening at the castle, and for the first time he thought it would be a good thing to marry. It was not only her thick, dark hair, her shining eyes and her graceful movement that enchanted him. It was her voice, her humour and her intelligence that captured Matholwch. Added to that, not only would marriage to her bring him a wife to provide him with beautiful heirs, it would give him power in Wales as well as in Ireland.

Branwen looked across the table at Matholwch, and saw that he stared at her.

She saw a tall man with a bush of red-gold hair and fine strong features. His lively, questioning blue eyes looked straight at her, and she blushed in confusion at first, but found herself returning his looks with smiles of encouragement as the evening progressed.

And as the two of them gazed at each other, all talk of war was forgotten. The whole company saw what was happening, though they did not refer to it, and it brought to the gathering a feeling of hope. A wedding between the two great houses of Ireland and Wales might resolve everything, and would it not be better for all than to continue with the warmongering, which had been going on for too long?

Matholwch asked the brothers for Branwen's hand in marriage, the very next day, and she, entranced by his red-gold hair and his witty way with words, told them she wished them to accept for her.

'You are sure?' Manawydan asked her. 'It means you will leave us and your home, to live with him in a land you know nothing of?'

'I am sure,' she pleaded. 'He is everything I have ever wanted in a husband. See how he gazes at me and already he talks of us having lovely children. I long to know his land and his people. Please, say yes for me.'

Bran was happy for his sister and also for his kingdom and, without reservation, he agreed.

'You have my blessing,' he said. 'He is the luckiest of men, to have found you for a wife. I will miss you, little sister, but it is gift from the fates that your marriage will bring us peace in our land. I am happy for you and for him.'

Manawydan, though, was unsure whether the Irish King was genuine in his affections. He wished to say as much but he could not bring himself to disappoint Branwen. She was so excited, and alight with the thought of marriage and the thrill of travelling to be Queen in Ireland.

'Let us give it seven days,' Manawydan said. 'For it is said that, on each day of the week, a man shows a different character of himself. And on the eighth day, if it is still your wish, we will see you married.'

Matholwch agreed to this and so the two spent a week getting to know each other. All went well and, as they wandered the castle lawns, or ate at table, or strolled on the beaches, everyone who saw them believed it was a union made in heaven, and on the eighth day, when Manawydan could say no more against it, they were wed.

It was a wonderful festive occasion. People from throughout

Bran's lands arrived at the castle with gifts, all of them delighted to witness this truly special marriage, which promised long-lasting peace between themselves and Matholwch of Ireland.

Bran watched the arrival of gifts and realised he had not thought what his own gift would be to the couple. Being a trusting soul, and perhaps carried away by the occasion and its huge impact on his countrymen, he decided he would provide a gift so unique and marvellous that Matholwch would hold him in respect for evermore.

The cauldron still sat undisturbed in its hidden room. Bran took two guards with him and unlocked the door, to inspect it. It had gathered dust but nothing more. He instructed them to polish it, to make it shine so that it looked like a gift fit for a king.

Bran's wise brother, Manawydan, did not know what Bran was intending until it was done. When Bran produced the cauldron as his parting gift, Manawydan is said to have let a sigh leave his lips that still moves on the wind in the Western lands to this very day. So deep was his horror and his sadness that he spent the night in invocations and meditations, desperately seeking intervention from the ancestors and the great spirits to avert the disaster he could so clearly foresee.

But his efforts were a waste of time.

Manawydan watched the great Irish ships sailing back to their own land the next day, with his sister on board along with the cauldron, and he wept for the stupidity of his brother Bran, and for the awful things that he knew would happen to the beautiful Branwen.

Branwen soon discovered she had married a man who was a greedy war-monger, and once she had produced an heir for him, he tired of her presence. She tried to please him but he scolded and shouted and treated her harshly.

Her laughter grew less, and she put all her time into nursing and caring for her baby, whilst Matholwch told her how he plotted to overthrow her brothers. He shouted at her for her foreignness, throwing food back at her if what she cooked for him did not please him. And, in the end, he cast her out from the hall alone, separating her from her tiny child.

She was forced to live in a dark pit beneath the kitchens where she washed and scrubbed day in and day out, with a violent man as her overseer.

Meanwhile, the cauldron, which had been given a place of importance on a high hill top overlooking the coastline, sat gleaming like silver from the constant polishing at the hands of Matholwch's men, who longed to try it out and discover its power.

Branwen, in desperation, talked to her only companion, a starling, who flew daily to sit on the edge of the pit. Each day she taught the bird a new word, and, bit by bit, to him she imparted her sadness, her pain, and her desire to see her brothers, and be rescued. And so it happened that one day, the bird flew across the sea, and communicated to Manawydan what he had been told.

As soon as the brothers heard what was happening to their sister, they set out to rescue her, bringing with them their half-brothers, the twins Nissen and Evnissen, and a whole army of fighting men, fit to take on the Irish.

They surprised the Irish King, who had no idea they had heard of his ill-treatment of their innocent sister, Branwen.

They came by night and snatched her from the pit before anyone had time to realise what was happening. But though she thanked her brothers with all her heart for rescuing her, Branwen refused to leave Ireland without her baby, and the baby was in the castle.

The Welsh managed by stealth to enter the castle, but it was with difficulty that they smuggled the baby out, and Matholwch, once alerted, was like a raging bull.

His fury made him gather a massive fighting force, and they went after Bran's men, determined to stop them from reaching their boats, and to kill all of them if necessary.

When they caught up with them, it was a terrible and bloody fight, The Irish steered the fighting away from the coast, keeping the Welsh troops inland, so they could not escape.

When darkness fell, the Welsh got a brief respite from the fighting, to tend their wounded and count their dead.

Across from where they camped they saw a fire take light on a hill nearby.

It was the fire beneath the cauldron, and as the bodies of the Irish dead were collected by their fellow-men, under Matholwch's orders, they were thrown into it.

By dawn the next day, as the Irish soldiers who watched drew back in horror, their unrecognisable undead brothers emerged. They climbed from the horrible pot, transformed by the unearthly flames. There was no flesh left on them, they were nothing but jerking bones, but they still carried their swords and knives, and they moved like machines, hacking all that came in their way.

The Welsh were taken unawares, overtaken by an enemy who did not tire, did not rest, did not think or feel, and, worst of all, did not go down in a fight without rising back to their feet.

Bran's foolish kindness in passing the cauldron to his wicked brother-in-law had brought the army of the undead in full horror to fight against him.

He spoke to his men, saying, 'If I had but known such hellish creatures could be brought to being from its burning heart, I would have thrown it back to the waves, to rest forever at the bottom of the sea. If we all die, then it is I who bear the blame, but we must fight to the end and get back to our boats, for nothing will stop these creatures from destroying every last one of us.'

The Irish King was so certain of their destruction that he laughed aloud at the horrors he saw, and left them to fight the undead, returning to his castle with his men, to celebrate their victory.

But just as the strength and the belief that they could ever win ebbed away from Bran's army, one of the half-brothers, the twin Evnissen, took matters into his own hands. Without a word, he ran from his Welsh brothers, up the hill, and leapt alive into the cauldron.

While it boiled the skin from his bones, he thrust out his hands and feet with all the force he could, pushing the walls of the cauldron in opposite directions. The brittle metal cracked and then, with a loud bang, it exploded, sending shards in all directions. The cauldron would never be used again.

The Welsh grieved for him and applauded his heroism, but the battle still raged, and now they were moving themselves, under Bran's good leadership, to get closer to the sea and their ships.

When they had put some distance between themselves and their enemy, Manawydan and Bran drew their followers around them, warily keeping watch for the Irish undead.

This time it was Manawydan who spoke to them. 'There is

only way to rescue these souls from eternal pain and deathless misery. We must drive them into the sea, into the arms of Neptune himself, from whose kingdom the cauldron was stolen. If Neptune takes pity on their souls, then, they will sink to the bottom of the ocean and the comfort of death will be theirs. They can make their journey to the land of Annwn, the land beyond death, and rest with their dead brothers and ancestors.'

Bran argued against him. 'Let us leave the undead to destroy Ireland for ever,' he said, 'to punish Matholwch. We are near enough to our boats to slip away.'

Many of the men agreed, but Manawydan shook his head. 'The Cauldron came from us,' he said sadly. 'In the eternal kingdoms, we will be judged as guilty as Matholwch himself for this disaster. We must do what we can to save these souls and our own.'

Reluctantly, the men agreed. Manawydan was wise, and they feared for their own souls, at his words.

So, Bran stood back whilst Manawydan gave instructions to the men, and they scattered, each to their allotted hiding place, the better to lure the undead warriors into the sea.

The zombie army came screaming towards them across the dunes, in terrifying inhuman unison, full only of one intent, to destroy. The rattling of their bones and the stench of burning filled the air.

One by one, the hidden men appeared, moving closer to the sea's edge, drawing the undead on, until they were all on the beach.

Manawydan did all in his power to guide the undead into the sea, whilst Bran himself stood, a Giant in the waves, beckoning them to a peaceful home in Neptune's arms.

He taunted them. 'Come and get me!' he bellowed. 'Come and destroy the King of Cymru, if you will...' and he laughed and jeered at them, and they ran into the sea with a fury that stopped them from seeing that they chased him to their death.

A great tidal wave swelled behind Bran, throwing him upward and enveloping the skeletons in one great flood of water. So powerful was the wave that Bran landed on the beach, whilst the horde of undead disappeared beneath the foaming sea.

Bran's army fell down on their knees. 'The great Sea God himself has saved us. Praise Neptune for his mercy and his power!' they cried.

They waited then for hours, to see if the undead would return, and as they loitered on that beach, thinking that they were alone, they were watched.

The eyes of three, who had not followed their brothers into the sea, followed everything they said and did. These three had been in the process of being transformed, when the cauldron had been destroyed, and were half alive, and half undead. Their minds were still sharp, and the damage of the cauldron had turned their brains to destructive and evil thoughts.

They waited, out of sight, as Bran's guards watched for any sign of the undead rising from the sea. None did, but Manawydan sensed the presence of the three who were left. He sent out parties of men to search the dunes, but the shadows were too deep for worthwhile search.

'There are some of them left, I know it,' he said. 'My skin crawls with the knowledge that the undead are still walking.'

But though they searched, they could not find the last three undead, who were hidden in the thickets of gorse, which grew on the dunes. And before dawn, when the tide came to its full height,

Neptune threw waves as tall as castles, to uproot them and bring them to their resting place, but even though he sent his Vimbligs, the wasps of the otherworld, who stung them ferociously, the undead clung screaming to the earth, and would not go.

The men could not get near them, and began to mutter that they should catch the tide.

Manawydan cried aloud for help from the gods. He knew, as only a seer could know, that if these three were left to wander between life and death, they would do any evil. He knew where their power lay and that they would spend their days stealing the dreams of men.

But though he prayed and cried, the tide and the wind were right for sailing home. Bran and all his men were anxious to leave and forget the three.

'We leave them in Ireland,' said Bran. 'Let Matholwch worry about them!'

And he led his men on to the ships.

Manawydan tried to explain how dangerous the undead were, that they were no longer contained in truly human form and could travel between the boundaries of dimensions unknown to men. But no-one wanted to know. They wanted to leave; to put behind them the terrible things they had seen, and return home to their loved ones, and to their own hearth.

'It rests in Neptune's great hands,' said Manawydan at last to Bran, his sadness creasing his wise face. 'The men are right. We cannot wait. We must take our sister and our loyal people home to safety, while we can.'

The great Welsh boats, filled with the tired and wounded Welsh army, slipped one by one out to sea, their progress watched by three pairs of red eyes in the thicket of gorse.

Manawydan saw them, a glimpse, then, nothing. His spirit was low.

'They can never die,' he said to Bran. 'They have escaped undeath and death, and are now free to move through this and other worlds. They can hide in the dreams of people anywhere, take whatever shape they will in their fantasies, steal their good dreams and, in their place, sow nightmare and chaos.'

Bran hung his head. He knew that if he had done as his brother had counselled and thrown the cauldron back into the ocean, none of the horrors they had seen or created in Ireland would have happened.

But Manawydan knew his feelings and he gave brotherly comfort. 'Matholwch was to blame, not you, brother. What you did, you did from kindness, and from a trusting heart. Take satisfaction in knowing one thing for certain, no man will ever find the cauldron and use its terrible power again.'

The first two books from the Dreamstealers trilogy...

The Fizzing Stone

Exciting contemporary fiction embroiled in ancient myths and Welsh legends. Will be enjoyed by all adventurous Harry Potter fans.

"Thrilling story... Nasty behaviour seems to indicate evil-doing, a familiar but always intriguing theme."
– **Hilary Cooper, www.gwales.com**

£5.95

ISBN: 0 86243 664 8

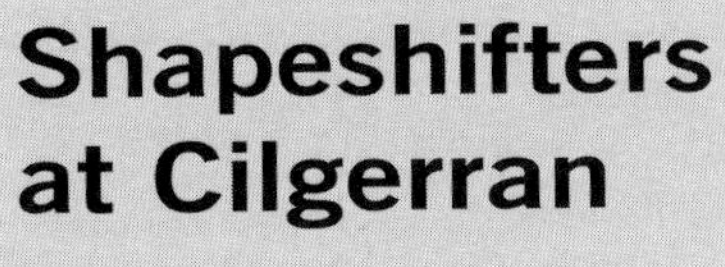

Shapeshifters at Cilgerran

Book two of the Dreamstealers trilogy. Join in Leo and Ginny's thrilling adventures as they are threatened again by the Dreamstealers.

"Beautifully written, full of twists and turns, well-drawn characters... with Whittaker's inimitable sense of humour, it is an enjoyable and gripping read."
– Amanda James, www.churchinwales.org

£5.95

ISBN: 0 86243 785 7